# HANSON

MEN OF BIRD'S EYE BOOK FOUR

KAT SAVAGE

This is a work of fiction. Names, characters, places, and incidents either are the product of the author's imagination or are used fictitiously. Any resemblance to actual persons, living or dead, events, or locales is entirely coincidental.

Copyright © 2022 by Kat Savage All rights reserved.

No part of this book may be reproduced or used in any manner without written permission of the copyright owner except for the use of quotations in a book review.

www.thekatsavage.com
thekatsavage@gmail.com

Cover Design by Kat Savage
Formatted by J.R. Rogue

*For my mother, who I miss with each passing day.
For every mother who longs to break the chains of their mistakes,
who prays they won't screw up their kids too badly in the process,
and to those still looking for the piece that makes their family whole.
Your Hanson is somewhere out there,
ready to step in and show you that not everyone leaves.*

## ALIEN BLUES

### HANSON

It's not that I don't love my therapist—I do. I really and truly do. But I have an intense disdain for the way he taps his pen on the side of his notepad while he's listening to me. If he wasn't such a good goddamn listener, I'd have probably taken it and stabbed him in the neck with it by now. Just kidding. But I would've thrown it out the open window behind him for sure.

Instead, I rationalize to myself that perhaps the source of his awesome listening powers is rooted in the way he taps that damn pen, and therefore stopping the tapping would render him useless. And I'd rather not start all over again with someone else. I didn't say my rationalizations were rational.

"Are you ready to talk about your father?" he asks.

Dr. Russell has been my therapist for two years. Every session, it's the same. We reach a natural point in which he asks this same question. And then I give the same response.

"Maybe next time, doc," I say.

"You're going to have to open up about him one of these days," he says.

"I know," I say.

"Give me something," he says. "One little thing."

My mind travels back to my childhood in Brazil. All I see when my mind goes back that far is my mother crying. There's also a lot of screaming. I try to go back further.

"His hands felt soft when he held mine despite all the times his knuckles were bloody," I say.

Dr. Russell quickly scribbles something on his notepad, which halts the tapping but my comment has piqued his special interest. That's probably the most I've told him about my father.

I talk about my mother all the time—her kindness, her intelligence, and the way she told me bedtime stories with character voices and props. Her pain. Her bruises at the hands of my father. How much I miss her. But my father? Salvador Juan Serrano is not a man I miss or care to talk about.

"Why were his knuckles usually bloody?" the doc asks.

I roll my neck. This chair is wildly uncomfortable. My fingertips grip the stiff armrests as I mull his question over.

"Maybe next time, doc," I say.

What I like most about Dr. Russell is that when I say I'm done, he doesn't push. So, he nods understandingly and begins to tap his pen again.

"You're going to have to trust someone eventually, Hanson," he says.

"Why?" I ask.

"Because you can't carry all that darkness yourself," he says. "Eventually you'll need someone to help you carry it."

Maybe he's right. Then again, maybe not. I've been successfully carrying the burden of my father's memory all my life and no one has helped me so far. Well, that's not entirely true. My mother shielded me from it until she couldn't anymore.

The doc and I shake hands and part ways at the end of my session, and I exit past his receptionist just like I do every Wednesday. We have a standing weekly appointment for ten in the morning. Luckily, my boss accommodates this. Hell, it was his idea to start therapy in the first place.

I'll admit I don't think I've made a lot of headway with Dr. Russell. The one thing he wants me to talk about is the one thing I avoid talking about like it's the goddamn plague. Still, he presses me to think differently about many things. I dish about work, my nearly nonexistent dating life, and pour through fifty different scenarios for my future. He asks questions and lends perspective I don't have.

I arrive at work at Bird's Eye Tattoo Studio to find everyone in a bit of a panic. Will is running around, Drew is nowhere to be found, Hawk is running out the back door, and Jericho has a person in his chair but the needle isn't going.

"What's going on?" I ask, my general direction toward Will.

"Hawk's mom fell and broke her hip!" Will yells back.

"Oh shit, is she okay?" I ask.

"I think she will be but Drew and Hawk are going to the hospital now, and then I don't know. I have to call all of

Hawk's appointments and pick up Ava from school in two hours and I also have people coming in to interview for the two piercing positions," she says.

She's losing it. Hell, so am I, a little. But I'll keep that on the inside for now. This also probably means that her boyfriend, Derek, is rushing to the hospital. Not only is Derek a doctor, and Will's boyfriend, but he's also Hawk's brother. Honestly, it's a lot to keep up with.

"Calm down," I say. "Give me half the list of people you need to call. And I'll pick up Ava from school and hang out with her upstairs until you're all back. You should go to the hospital after the interviews to be there for everyone."

Because my therapy appointments are on Wednesdays, I never book clients. I only take walk-ins for the rest of the day so I have plenty of time to help. Will has been in their lives since childhood so I know she will want to be there.

"Are you sure?" she asks, a look of desperation in her eyes.

"Of course," I say. "That woman is more a mother to you than your mother. Go be there for her and Hawk and Derek."

After she agrees with only a hint of reluctance, we head back to the office, where she splits the list with me. This is the one day Hawk was booked from open to close with lots of little tattoos but we manage to get through it without anyone yelling at us. You never know what you're going to get with people, but almost everyone we've tattooed is chill as fuck.

"Okay, I'm going to contact the piercers and get them in here early if I can, then I'm taking off," Will says. "Are you sure you can get Ava?"

"Yeah, of course," I say. "I know Drew put all of us on her

pick-up list back when she was pregnant with Knox so I'll be fine. Wait, who's got the baby?"

"He's in daycare," she says. "He can stay there a bit later and they'll pick him up on the way home. Or if they need to be there longer, I will get him."

"Cool, okay. Sounds like we have a vague plan," I laugh.

I run back out to the front while she gets on the phone with the interviewees. Since no one is here to man the front counter, I take a seat on the stool there to answer the phone and look at the appointment calendar.

"Hey, man," Jericho calls from his booth. "This is the only appointment I have today, so I'll be fine when everyone leaves."

"Okay, cool," I say. "I'm not worried."

I know he's saying that because he's only worked here a few months, but I trust him. I've known him for a long time and suggested him when a spot opened up. Avery, the guy he replaced, is one of my best friends. But he went and fell in love with a billionaire—no I'm not kidding—and is now running the second Bird's Eye location down in Nashville. Sure, it's only a couple of hours to drive from here in Louisville. And sure, Jericho is a cool guy. But I'll be the first to admit I miss that dude—even if we text every day.

# LITTLE POOR ME
## THEA

I wonder how many times I will repeat to myself that it's Wednesday, which means it's closer to the weekend than not. I also wonder how many times this class is going to make me repeat the same steps to the same math problem that's been written on the whiteboard for twenty minutes.

"Miss James," says Ethan. "Which place do you subtract again?"

By my count, that's fifteen. Fifteen times I've explained various portions of the problem.

"Let's just do it all together," I say, finally succumbing to insanity and walking to the board.

I grab a marker and show the kids step by step so we can do it as a group. Once we're done, it's as if they all seem to totally understand. Sixth graders are so fracking frustrating.

"Now, everyone take out their homework logs and be sure to study for your test this Friday," I say.

"Miss James?" Ava asks. "Will this problem be on the test?"

"Not this exact one, but several like it," I say. "Study unit six in your textbook and you should do great."

Ava isn't a student I have to worry about. She has excellent grades in all her classes. My son, Ethan, on the other hand... well, let's just say it will be a miracle if I can get him through sixth-grade math.

Don't get me wrong, my son is smart. He loves reading and writing and has excellent grades in history too. But math and science aren't his strong suits and we work hard at home to make sure he learns what he needs to maintain decent grades.

Wednesday also means Ethan goes to his father's for the night. Don't get me wrong, I love my son, but the mid-week break is sometimes much needed. I often use my time without him to see friends or go on dates, and several other things I don't do when he's with me. For the record, he's with me ninety-five percent of the time. Shane—my ex and baby daddy—isn't exactly reliable. Despite having paperwork that clearly outlines visitation, he still misses a lot of his days. And honestly, some nights he's with his father, I just drink a glass of wine and fall asleep on the couch at seven.

Not tonight, though. Tonight, I have a date. I'd stopped trying for a while but now I'm back on the saddle. Or back in the pond. Or ready to sew some oats. Whatever people say. Notice I didn't say "wild oats". My wild days are behind me. I had enough of that with Shane.

"Miss James," a boy in the back named Theodore calls, snapping me back.

"Yes?" I ask.

"Will the problem we just went over be on the test?" he asks.

Lord help me. I redirect the class to begin their worksheets and sit at my desk to review my lesson plans for next week. Checking my phone, I notice a message from Shane, and two more from Clint, my date for tonight.

**SHANE: I'll be there at release.**

Why he felt the need to tell me that is beyond me. That's what time he's supposed to be here anyway. The deal is he picks Ethan up from me at the school when it lets out.

I move on to the messages from Clint without answering Shane.

**CLINT: We still on for six? Still good with Rizzo's?**
**CLINT: Can't wait to meet you**

A little flutter travels through my chest as I feel the first wave of first date jitters.

I type back a reply, confirming and telling him the feeling is mutual before shoving my phone back in my desk drawer. Clint is exactly the kind of guy I need in my life. He's stable and has an actual career even if it does sound dreadfully boring. I'm not even quite sure I understand it, but he seems to be passionate about it so who am I to judge? The point is, he's nothing like my ex, who bounced from a dead-end job to "gig" work back to another dead-end job and once invested our rent money in a pyramid scheme.

I blame my falling for him on his singing voice. Because

even though he used to chain smoke cigarettes, his voice melted me. I'm fairly certain he's the male version of a siren, luring unknowing immature women to their demise one sweet note at a time. Between the voice, the grunge style clothes, and the tattoos, I was a twenty-three-year-old goner. Eleven years later, I would not and will not be making the same mistakes.

"Miss James?" Someone calls out and it takes me a full ten seconds to bring the class into focus.

"Sorry, guys, I was a little distracted," I say. "Is everyone finished with their worksheet?"

"Are you okay?" A girl named Sara asks.

"I'm fine, yes," I say.

All the kids are staring at me like I've grown a second head. Not that I blame them. Their teacher just went full-on robot in shutdown mode at her desk, getting lost in thoughts of her spotty youth.

Exactly four seconds later, the bell rings. I find myself quite literally saved by the bell.

## BOOM CLAP

### HANSON

There's a homeless man who sits on the corner of the road near the shop. If you walk to Ava's school from this direction, you pass him. His name is Anthony, though I'm probably the only one in a ten-mile radius who knows that. I drop a few dollars into his cup and he nods silently. Truth be told, I don't use or carry cash for any reason other than to make sure I can give him a few bucks when I see him. We've spoken before, but not this time and not most times. It's just a quiet understanding and moment of gratitude. On both our parts.

When I was a child in Brazil, my mother would take me into the heart of poor areas and we would pass out water and food. My father called her Mother Theresa like it was an insult, though I didn't realize it at the time.

Approaching the school, I see a slew of cars lined up, parents eager and annoyed with the process of long lines like there's some other way. It makes me feel glad to be on foot. I glide right up to the door where walking students will come out and see only two adults waiting there. Of course, they both make eyes at me like I'm a leper. The lady nearest to me even adjusts the strap of her purse, clutching it closer as if I might rob her.

Sometimes this world has a skewed perception of the person under the ink. Don't worry, Karen, I don't want your knock-off Michael Kors bag. Normally, in situations like this, I'd try to break the tension with a joke or some sort of relatable topic so they can see that I'm a real boy, but I'm not in the mood today.

The loudest chime in the world dings from a speaker right above my head, sending a wave of rage down my spine. I make a note never to stand in this particular spot ever again. As if perfectly choreographed, children begin pouring out from all the exits, some boarding buses, others climbing into cars, and several out of the door next to me who scatter in all walking directions.

Ava and a boy file out together, talking and laughing before she spots me.

"Hanson!" She comes running in my direction, the boy following just behind her.

"*Olá, princesa,*" I say. She's never been a big fan of me calling her a princess, but it's sort of a joke between us now. She's forever the princess of Bird's Eye and the matter is not open for debate.

"This is my friend, Ethan," she says, pointing at the boy.

"*Olá,* Ethan," I say.

"Whoa," he says. "I like your accent."

"Hanson is from Brazil," Ava chimes in.

Ethan looks at me like an exotic animal. If he were an adult, it would be annoying, but the pure innocence of childhood curiosity causes me to lean into my character.

*"Espero que você teve um bom dia,"* I say, Ethan's eyes wide and fully captivated.

"That means he hopes we had a good day," Ava says.

She's been catching onto common words and frequent phrases and I say this to her every day when she gets to the shop. Of course, she's not conversational yet, but we've got time. If I have anything to do with it, she'll be bilingual before she hits college.

"Cool," he exclaims. "Oh, there's my mom."

He gestures behind me, so I turn abruptly, not realizing his mother is much closer than I anticipated. My sudden movement knocks her off balance and she goes tumbling backward to the ground. I wish I could say it was one of those slow-motion moments where I find myself reaching out to catch her in the nick of time, but it wasn't like that at all.

It was a flash of flailing arms and fire-red hair and a crash. I think the only emotion registering on my face is stunned silence.

"Oh my god," I say. "I'm so sorry."

"Jesus," she exclaims, attempting to wipe the mulch from her legs. Did I mention she fell back halfway into a manicured bush surrounded by mulch? "Do you have a modicum of awareness?"

Modicum? Don't hear that word too often.

"Let me help you," I say, reaching down. Her face is obscured by her wavy red hair, now tousled in all directions.

"I can do it," she says, more than a hint of frustration in her tone.

I can't do anything more than stand, patiently waiting for her to right herself, to maybe make eye contact. Her hands come to either side, hoisting her bottom from the ground. Once onto her feet, she's still looking down at the many pieces of mulch clinging to her stockings. I will thank the gods that her skirt is long enough that this didn't turn into a peep show.

"Can I get you anything?" I ask.

"No, I think you've done quite enough," she says.

As the last word of her statement falls from her mouth, she finally looks up at me, pushing her hair behind her ears. Whoa.

Her high cheekbones and the bridge of her nose are covered in freckles, contrasting against her pale skin which only accentuates the green flecks in her hazel eyes. I find myself swallowing for no good reason at all.

"*Olá*," I say. "I mean, hello."

"Oh, um, hi," she says, seemingly just as startled as I am. She blinks rapidly for another few seconds before acknowledging the kids.

"Ethan," she says. It's not a question. It's not the start of a sentence, but merely a realization that's why she was coming over in the first place. Or at least that's the way it seems.

"I'm sorry, who are you?" She turns back to me.

"This is Hanson," Ava says.

"I'm sort of her uncle," I explain.

"Not sort of, Hanson," Ava says. "You are totally my uncle."

My heart does a little flutter at her correction. If Ava does anything for all the misfits I work with, she has a subtle way of softening us, of making us realize we're more than the discarded toys we think of ourselves as.

I give the woman half a smile and extend my hand. "Nice to meet you."

"This is Miss James," Ava says. "My math teacher."

"And Ethan's mother," Miss James adds.

"Oh, okay," I say. "I work with Hawk and Drew at the tattoo shop."

There's a touch of relief in Miss James's eyes as she begins to piece everything together.

"Nice to meet you," she says, placing her hand in mine.

And though I'm surprised by her acceptance of it, given I just knocked her over, I'm grateful she's treating me like a human and not a sideshow.

"I'm sorry, again, for knocking you over. I didn't realize you were that close," I say.

"It's fine," she says. "No big deal."

I'm compelled by nothing other than the small scar above the right corner of her mouth to know more about her.

"Maybe I can make it up to you," I suggest.

"What do you mean?" she asks, her voice laced with hesitation.

"Can I take you to dinner sometime? Tonight maybe?" I ask.

If there was any confusion about my intentions before, they're registering loud and clear now and she doesn't look quite as excited as I'd hoped.

"Oh, um, thank you for the offer, but I can't. I have plans tonight," she says.

"She has a date," Ethan blurts out.

"Ethan," she says, her head snapping in his direction. Her tone is the one only ever heard from mother to child, the one that silences and warns all at once.

I can't help but smile at the exchange. "Well, maybe another night?"

"No, really, I don't think so," she says.

"Hey," a man's voice interrupts us, Miss James turning first.

"Dad!" Ethan exclaims, running toward the man.

Ahh, the dad. Okay, cool. The two hug for a moment as he walks up, looking from Miss James to me and back again.

"Hey," she says to him. "His bag is in my car."

"Who's this?" he asks, looking at me. "Your date?"

His tone isn't rude but there's a hint of concern. The guy has several visible tattoos on his arms, almost as heavily tattooed as I am but he's seen his way around the needle more than a few times.

"This is Ava," she says. "My student and Ethan's friend. This is Hanson, Ava's uncle."

She ignores the part about being her date and instead sticks to what's relevant. I like that.

"Hey, man," I say, extending my hand in his direction.

He shakes it firmly. "Nice ink," he says.

"Thanks, man," I say. "I'm a tattoo artist down the road so I guess you could say I have a lot of talented friends."

"Really?" he says. "I've been looking for a new artist to work with. Got a card?"

I pull one from my front pocket. I always have a few on me for this very reason. And while this exchange seems to be making Miss James uncomfortable, she remains silent until we're done.

"The door to my car is unlocked," she says, as if to dismiss him. "Ethan, I'll see you tomorrow, okay?"

Ethan nods, walking toward the parking lot with his dad, leaving just the two of us and Ava behind.

"Sorry about that," she says, as if there's something to apologize for. "What was I saying? Oh right, I'm sorry but I can't go out with you. I don't think it would be appropriate."

"Is that the real reason?" I tease, laughing.

Something about her posture and her ex's appearance makes me think otherwise. And despite her reluctance, she answers honestly.

"No," she says. Her eyes travel down to Ava, who's being a naturally nosy kid and I take the hint.

"Ava, can you give us just a minute?" I ask.

Ava pulls her headphones out of her bag, places them over her head, and walks a few paces away, pulling out her phone and sitting down against the building. After she's picked a song, she'll pull out her sketchbook and care less what's going on.

Miss James presses her lips into a line, then licks the top one.

"I don't think it would be a good idea," she says. "Besides, it's true. I'm going on a date tonight. And even though it's the first date, I think it's promising so I'll probably be going on more dates with him."

"What's his name?" I ask.

My question throws her, and I'll admit it's probably not in line with the usual exchange.

"Clint," she says.

I wrinkle my nose. "I don't know. You're not giving me Clint energy."

"What does that mean?" she asks.

"It means I just don't see you with a Clint, that's all," I say, shrugging.

"Okay, well, that's a bit presumptuous, don't you think?" she counters.

"What's your ex's name?" I ask.

"What?" she says. "Why?"

"Just proving a point," I say.

"It's Shane," she says.

"Ah, yeah," I say. "He was probably a wild one, huh?"

"Yes," she says, heavy emphasis on the word and all its implications.

"Which tells me you need a little something more than a Clint can provide you," I say. "But also a little more reliability than Shane provided you."

Miss James crosses her arms over her chest, a clear sign that what I'm saying hits too close to home.

"Enter Hanson," I say, smiling.

"I've had my share of bad boys," she says. "I think I'll pass."

"What's wrong with a bad boy?" I ask.

"Where do I start?" she says, her arms flailing. "First, they quite literally charm your pants off. They bring you flowers and take you on nice dates and maybe even chocolates and a dumb teddy bear. And you're thinking, wow, this is great, totally unexpected. Then they completely flip the script and become exactly what you were worried they were. Don't hold down a job, play gigs in different cities on the weekend and swear the girls are just fans of the band."

I listen without interrupting because her experiences are valid and I'm just a man who hasn't lived it. And I can see her story playing in my head like a movie as she goes on, no doubt telling the story of her and Shane and the reasons she's now a single mom. I get it.

She finishes speaking with a huff, catching her breath after the long-winded speech.

"Well," I say. "I can't argue with that."

"Exactly," she says. "It's nothing personal, I just have to think about what's best for me at this point in my life."

"That's understandable," I say. "You have a kid after all."

"Right," she says. She seems thrown off guard again, this time by how agreeable I'm being.

I'm not one of those men who push. At least not the way most men do. Her eyes study my face, like maybe she's waiting for me to say something.

"And anyway, I think you're probably much too young for me," she says. "You don't look like you're even thirty."

"I'm not," I say, plainly.

"Wow," she says. "Yeah, definitely too young. Another red flag."

"Age is important to you?" I ask.

"When you're a thirty-three-year-old single mother, yeah. It's important," she says.

I tuck away all these morsels of information into a new file in my head. You can know a lot about a person without knowing much at all. You just have to pay attention. There's one thing I still don't know, though.

"Can I ask one more question?" I say.

"What?" she says.

"Do you have a first name or should I keep calling you Miss James?" I laugh.

She presses her eyes closed for a second, the ghost of a smile on her mouth.

"Thea," she says. "My name is Thea."

"*Olá*, Thea," I say, extending my hand one last time. "It's so nice to meet you."

Her freckled skin blushes the most subtle pink shade as she smiles.

"It's nice to meet you, too, Hanson," she says. "And I wish you all the best luck finding someone your age or maybe who would be into what you're offering."

I nod my head wondering all the while if she means what she's saying. On the surface, she probably does. I think deep down, though, it might be different.

"Well then, I hope your date with Clint goes well and he's what you're looking for," I say. "Maybe I'll see you around."

I wave at Ava, who stands and starts toward us. I look Thea James in the eyes one more time, then turn toward the shop with Ava at my side.

Maybe I should leave it alone, let the whole thing be. Maybe I have no business being interested in an older, single mom who has a prejudice.

A male lion cannot join a pride until the female lions accept him. They decide if he is worthy and he must prove himself. I don't think he does this by strong-arming them. To win the grace of the lioness feels like a worthy endeavor.

And I like a good challenge.

## OVERKILL

### THEA

Two dresses hang on the backside of my closet door, and neither is really wowing me. The first is a lace black number, hugging my chest and curves all the way to my knees. The other is yellow satin, and though that sounds an odd choice, it pairs nicely with my skin tone. The skirt is less snug, but what it lacks in tightness it makes up for in cleavage.

Honestly, either would probably be fine. But somewhere throughout the day, I lost my enthusiasm for this date. Perhaps it was while going over the same math problem fourteen times. Or maybe it was when I ran out of one hundred-calorie pack of Oreos in my desk drawer. It could be the moment Shane's stupid face showed up. He always rains on my parade.

But no. Who am I kidding? I know exactly when my panties got knotted. Ava's uncle, Hanson, was quite a surprise. Although, based on what Drew told me about the tattoo shop during a parent-teacher conference, I shouldn't be all that shocked. At the time, I was happy that she and Ava found a family to call their own. She's filled me in about Ava's father, Hawk's new role, and anything about Ava's home life because it's helpful for teachers to know this going on.

However, she failed to mention one tiny detail by the name of Hanson—uncle Hanson. And by "tiny detail" I mean one smokin' hot Brazilian bad boy who is the epitome of every bad decision I ever made in my twenties.

Why would she? It's not like I introduce myself with, "Hi, I'm Miss James, your kid's sixth-grade math teacher. I like long walks on the beach, shitty tattooed bad boys who treat me like dirt, and I don't think I've ever had an orgasm in all my thirty-three years on this earth."

God, even just thinking it makes me sigh. That's right. No orgasms. At least not by any of my lovers. Sure, I can pull one off myself now and then but that's rather disheartening.

I finally yank the black lace number off my closet door and pull it over me in a huff. Focus, Thea. You've got a good date ahead of you. Don't get derailed by repeating the same mistakes. You shaved your legs for this.

About a half-hour later, I've managed to finish getting ready and even threw a little vanilla extract on my pulse points. Ladies, take my advice. A touch of vanilla along with your perfume is like a magic spell.

There's a knock at my door no sooner than I finish slipping my feet into heels. He's on time. Check.

Opening the door, I plaster on my most impressive smile and say a silent prayer.

"Thea?" he asks, as if he's forgotten the photos on my dating profile entirely.

Though, if I'm reading his reaction right, he's not upset about what's standing in front of him. He makes no secret out of his roaming gaze.

"Hi, you must be Clint, it's nice to finally meet you in person," I say, extending my hand for a cursory official handshake. His hands aren't sweaty. Check.

"These are for you," he says, presenting a bouquet of pink roses from behind him.

"Thank you so much," I say. "Let me just lay them in the sink."

He has good taste. Check.

A few minutes later, we're in his car on the way to a restaurant he chose and I take note of its cleanliness. Not a slob. Check. I know it sounds ridiculous but my checklist is a necessary dating tool at this point. It keeps me focused on what's important to me and pushes out the noise aka my inner rebellious voice from my youth beckoning me to be bad again. That girl is long gone.

"So," I say, poised to begin chatting to distract from my internal thoughts. "I apologize if this sounds dense, but what exactly is it you do?"

Clint laughs. "Don't apologize, it's not the first time I've had to further explain it."

"Oh good," I say, sighing with relief.

"It's all numbers and data points. I won't bore you with what all the numbers and data mean, but we use it to analyze market trends and supply that information to our clients so they can accurately project their next business quarter."

I get that he just explained it, I do. But I still don't fucking get it. He continues blurting out various aspects of his job as I try hard to concentrate, but if you've ever seen any of the memes where the person's face is completely blank while math symbols float around their head, I imagine that's what I look like right now.

But as I stated before, I don't have to understand it. He seems to know what he's talking about and makes a nice living and that's all that matters to me.

Clint laughs at something he's said, and I get the feeling it's less a generalized joke and more like one of those jokes only the people he works with would understand and laugh at. Nevertheless, I make an effort at a slight chuckle out of courtesy.

"And you teach sixth grade?" he asks. "How's that?"

"Yes, math," I say. "And I do love it. Sure, the kids can get a little crazy sometimes but at the end of the day, I enjoy feeling like I'm helping them prepare for life."

"Is it what you always wanted to do?" he asks.

"No," I admit. "When I was younger, I had a pretty wild imagination and thought I was going to be the lead singer of an all-girl punk band."

My tone is so matter-of-fact that I can tell Clint doesn't know whether to laugh like I'm joking or inquire further.

"I'm kidding," I lie. He finally laughs and I make a note in the negative column. It's a little thing. But the idea that I don't feel like I can be honest and tell him that's really what I wanted seems like a step in the wrong direction, especially this early on.

I want to be able to tell someone everything about myself without fear of judgment or ridicule. And Clint seems like the type of put-together guy who wouldn't appreciate my youthful indulgences. Which is kind of a bummer.

## MANIC

### HANSON

Will and Derek arrive back at Hawk's place with the baby in tow, the pair of them looking utterly exhausted.

"What's the word?" I ask.

Derek pulls two beers from the fridge and hands one to Will. Given neither of them are heavy drinkers, this must mean things aren't great.

After Derek takes a couple of slugs, he sits it down, wiping the back of his hand over his upper lip.

"Mom's gonna need surgery. That's tomorrow morning. I know the surgeon, he's good. So I'm not worried. Then she will be in the hospital for about five days before she can go home. Once home, she's going to need someone there to help her for several weeks. It will be three to six months before she's well again."

"Wow," I say. "That's rough. What's the plan?"

"Derek and I are going to stay here with Hawk and Drew to help with the baby and Ava in the evenings. We were hoping you could continue to drop Ava off at school and pick her up?" Will's words are pointed in my direction and a bell dings over and over in my mind.

"Definitely," I say, trying not to sound too excited about it but also wondering how long it's going to take me to wear Thea James down.

"Great," Derek says. "Hawk and I are going to take turns helping Mom. It will be easier for us to lift her if needed."

"Smart," I say. "Let me whip you guys up something to eat." I push past them in the kitchen.

"Oh you don't have to," Will starts.

"Nonsense," I say. "I already fed Ava and we went over her homework. The baby still looks to be asleep so if you want to put him in his crib, I'll warm up something for you."

"You're a lifesaver, man," Derek says, cupping his hand on my shoulder as he retreats with Will down the hallway.

Honestly, it's the least I can do. Being in a hospital all day is draining. I'm not sure why since you're mostly just sitting there, but it takes it out of you. Plus, Momma Tanner is like a mom to all of us. We go to cookouts at her house and for holidays. This is a group effort.

A few minutes later, they emerge and sit at the bar just in time for me to sit some plates down in front of them.

"It's not much," I say. "But it's pretty good."

"Hanson," Will says. "This looks amazing. How long were we gone?"

I laugh. "Long enough."

I've been cooking for myself for a long time. If I learned anything, it's that unless you want to eat ramen every day, you'd better get good at cooking. And when I first came to America, I had like no money, so I got pretty good at making something out of nearly nothing.

"Is this ham?" Derek asks.

"Yeah, grilled ham and cheese, with a little pickle and mustard," I say. "Fried a couple of slices of potato on the side."

Derek takes another large bite, seemingly satisfied with everything. I also really love feeding people. Something is satisfying about elevating someone's mood using food. It's like a hug for their stomach. It's better than a regular hug but not as good as sex.

"So there's this woman," I blurt out.

Both of them stop chewing, their eyes growing wide. I don't know why I said that. It's going to be a whole thing now.

"Like as in a woman you're interested in?" Will asks.

But her tone gives her away. She's suppressing a heavy amount of excitement. Her pretend calm could use some work.

"Yes," I say.

"Since when?" Derek asks.

"Since today," I say. "It's Ava's math teacher. Her name is Thea James."

"So did you ask her out or something?" Will asks.

"I tried," I huff. "Walked away with the sting of rejection."

"What? But you're like, awesome," Derek says.

I nod, agreeing with his statement. It's not that I'm trying to be arrogant, but I am confident. On the rare occasion I do approach a woman, I'm not usually rejected. I can't remember a time before today.

"She's older than me," I say.

"So?" Will says.

"So, I think she thinks it's a bad idea. If I had to guess, she's maybe six or seven years older. And she has a son."

"You're great with kids, though," Will says. "She's missing out. Screw age. It means nothing."

I nod again, completely in agreement about the age thing and the fact that she has a son. Neither bothers me. I wonder why they bother her? And after seeing her ex, I think it may be that I remind her too much of him. Shane's in good shape, heavily tattooed, and would fit right in if he walked in the door at Bird's Eye. Hell, maybe it's a combination of all those things.

"I think I'm going to try again," I say. "Not in a creepy stalker way. I don't want to badger her. I have to be subtle about it."

"I think that's a good idea," Derek says. "Show her what you're about."

The sound of my foot tapping against the hardwood floor becomes more prevalent as I sink further into my thoughts. The sounds of Will and Derek eating and talking to one another fades until it's only muffled background noise. Sometimes I get like this when I'm tattooing. All I can see is the canvas of skin in front of me. I only hear the buzz of the machine. It's a very specific sort of bliss.

I think back to my conversation with Thea, attempting to remember what she said about bad boys and how they "charm your pants off". My best play is to prove to her I'm not the kind of guy she thinks I am.

Now, if I can just figure out how the fuck to do that.

# NONFICTION

## THEA

There's a small table in the corner of the teachers' break room that has a wobbly leg. It's only really large enough for one person so anytime I can, this is where I sit. I adjust my laptop, the table tilting in response before leveling back out. I don't mind it. Especially because it means I can put my earbuds in and ignore everyone.

It's not that I dislike my colleagues. They're very nice people. But for whatever reason, this school lacks teachers under the age of fifty. Almost everyone here is so much older than me, it's like talking to my parents. They all try to give me parental advice and attempt to invade my personal life like it's their job to guide me through life. I know they're just trying to be nice but it's overwhelming most of the time. So, I stick to my one-man wobbly table.

I've got about forty-five minutes until my next class and like most days, I don't get to take a break during this time. I'm always working on lesson plans and other things. Occasionally, though, I get to work on my passion project. No one knows about it but I've been secretly writing a book. I've always wanted to and I've had this idea in my mind for years so I finally decided to give it a shot.

That's what I'm working on today for at least a few minutes. Though, I'm having a difficult time concentrating. Every few minutes I review different parts of my date with Clint last night. It's crucial to me that I choose a partner that's good for me and Ethan. I refuse to live the life I did ten years ago. And even though it's been that long, I've only introduced Ethan to maybe two or three of the men I've dated. Call me crazy, but I'm just really cautious.

My phone vibrates next to me, and Clint's name pops up on the screen as I reach for it.

**CLINT: I had a really good time with you last night.**
**CLINT: I was hoping we could do it again?**

My fingers hover over the keys as I contemplate my answer. Honestly, I'm torn. He's a good guy. He's stable and has a reliable career. He's not bad-looking. Truthfully, he's not physically what I would go for but it's not bad. Then again, what I used to go for is what got me in trouble. Maybe I can get used to it?

**ME: Sure, I'd love to. When were you thinking?**
**CLINT: This Saturday night?**
**ME: That sounds good to me.**

Fortunately, this is also Shane's weekend to have Ethan. Although, it's not even an entire weekend, in my opinion. He picks Ethan up just before dinnertime on Saturday and then brings him home Sunday night. Sometimes he will keep him until Monday morning and drop him off at school, but not often.

**CLINT:** Let me work out the details and I'll get back to you.

**ME:** Sounds good.

**CLINT:** Hope you have a great day :)

Well, that's sweet. Though, I'll admit he sounds more excited than I do. I don't know. I have a couple of days to think it over.

The bell rings abruptly, startling me from my thoughts and cutting our conversation short. That damn bell is so loud. Every year, several of us petition to lower it a little but it's always rejected. Why? Mrs. Thompson is our eighty-three-year-old librarian. She also helps out in the media lab, and the front office, and she's a cafeteria monitor. Mrs. Thompson also happens to be very hard of hearing. So the bell is set extra loud to afford her the ability to feel it. Of course, after this was explained to us earlier this year, we stopped petitioning for it.

Nevertheless, the bell ringing also signals that I'm due in class five minutes from now. Gathering my things, I think ahead to when school lets out. It's a frequent daydream of mine. On several days and occasions, I literally cannot wait to get out.

Today, those daydream thoughts are a little different. They're still about the end of the day. But they hang on one question swirling in my mind. I wonder if Ava's uncle is picking her up again?

And then, I want to slap myself in the fucking face because

no way. Not a chance in hell. My mind is on board. My heart is on board. However, it's my lower bits... my lady button, if you will, that has another set of thoughts entirely. Very hot thoughts. Very inappropriate thoughts.

I can't blame her. She's a little starved at this point. I admit, with a great deal of shame, that it's been almost two years since I've had sex. And let me tell you, that's a long fucking time. Not to mention, with more shame, it's been even longer since I had an actual orgasm.

So yeah, my loins are burning. My lady button is ready to be pushed. And Hanson Serrano is exactly the kind of man I get lusty for. Because I'm an idiot. And I like repeating the same mistakes.

"Oh, Miss James," a voice calls to me as I exit the break room.

Principal O'Neal's voice is unmistakable. It's deep, carrying the faintest hint of a speech impediment. I find it endearing.

"Yes, sir?" I reply.

"Please, I've told you repeatedly to call me Patrick," he says.

I know that without him reminding me but I nod a silent "my bad" to move the conversation forward.

"Don't forget you wrote your name down on the volunteer list to chaperone the sixth-grade dance at the end of the month," he says. "And we're short on volunteers so if you know any parents who'd be interested, please send them my way."

"I haven't forgotten and I will do that," I say, knowing full well I don't know any parents interested in babysitting children who don't belong to them.

"Great," he says. "And please, stop calling me sir. I call my father sir. I can't be a sir yet."

I laugh, nodding in agreement. For me, it was never about his age. I was just trying to be respectful of his position. He's new this year, and very different from our last principal, who insisted on being called sir. Patrick is a little more laid back. He very much wants to be your friend. I guess I'm still getting used to the differences.

He clasps me on the shoulder as he departs from me down the hallway toward the front office. And I could swear his hand lingers a few fractions of a second longer than I expect.

Or perhaps, I've just become so horny every cursory touch feels like it could be the one to turn me into Niagara Falls. Jesus, I've got to get a hold of myself. I'm about to be in class with twenty eleven-year-olds for fuck's sake. If they detect even a hint of awkwardness, change in my tone, or any other lack of poker face, I'm done for.

Then again, if I don't remedy myself—and soon—I'm going to end up drinking an entire bottle of wine while I simultaneously update my dating profile and go on an online sex toy shopping spree where I'll max out my credit card in an effort to buy an orgasm.

## FALLING DOWN

### HANSON

There's a pep in my step today, I'll be the first to admit it. This morning, all our plans fell into place. I took Ava to school. Jericho and I opened the shop, and Will followed shortly after. She dropped the baby off at daycare. Derek went to work. Drew is at Momma Tanner's place making it recovery friendly. Hawk is at the hospital with his mom.

Honestly, it felt like it was going to be a lot. When you say it out loud, it seems that way. But aside from allowing for a little more time to do everything, I feel like we really nailed it as a team. Of course, it's only day one. I don't want to get too braggy.

Jericho and I spent the morning tattooing like usual. Hawk's appointments were moved off the calendar for the next few weeks, and everyone was pretty understanding. Will is now and has always been a fucking badass at running this shop, so Hawk knows it's in good hands.

I took my lunch break to run to the store and pick up a few things and now I'm off to pick up Ava. It's the part of the day I've been looking forward to the most if I'm being honest.

I approach the same door I did yesterday, a heavy brown paper bag tucked beneath my arm. I push the mess of hair on the left side of my face behind my ear and I wait. I'm good at waiting. If it were an Olympic sport, I'd have a fair shot at gold. Though, today, I'm a little antsy.

This is either the most brilliant plan I've ever had or it's colossally the exact opposite. It's a go big or go home situation if you know what I mean.

The bell rings, causing me to stand upright from my slouched position. I don't even know why I'm assuming Miss James comes out each day. Mostly, I'm just sort of hoping that's what she does. Otherwise, this plan is completely fucked and this heavy-ass bag is for nothing.

Students begin to pile out as I keep my eyes peeled for Ava. Despite my attention being split, she's still the priority here. But it doesn't take long to spot her with the boy from yesterday which plays in my favor. Ethan is Thea's son. That means she might be coming out. Score.

I wave to Ava just as she catches sight of me and the two meander through the crowd toward me.

"Hey, Hanson," Ava says.

*"Olá, princesa, como foi o seu dia?"* I ask.

This is a test. We've been practicing her Portuguese. She knows if I ask any question in it, she's supposed to reply in it. She pauses for a moment as she searches for the right words.

*"Tive um bom dia, e você?"* she says, her pronunciation better

than I'd have expected at this point. Sure, it doesn't seem like a lot. A very basic, "how was your day, mine was good, how was yours" exchange. But she hasn't been my student for all that long and I'm impressed.

"*Tem sido adorável, princesa,*" I reply.

Ava's face beams brightly. She's enjoyed being my student as much as I've enjoyed being her teacher.

"Wow," Ethan chimes in.

"Can you teach me too?" he asks.

I give a little laugh. "Sure, amigo. Anytime."

Ethan's face has a similar light-up reaction and I'm just now noticing his eyes are the same shade as his mother's. In fact, after meeting both of his parents, I see very little of his father in him, if any. The same thing could be said about me, and though I don't know how Ethan feels about it, I am relieved by it.

Moments later, Miss James appears at the doorway behind them, snagging my nearly full attention. Thea. When I say it in my mind, I like how it sounds. Here's hoping she does too.

Her eyes draw toward me and then the kids and then me again. She sees me. And she sees me seeing her. Still, she hesitates for a moment before walking over to us.

"Ah, Mr. Serrano," she says. "Good to see you again."

Eck. Mr. Serrano. For the love of God, just no.

"Please don't call me that," I say. "Mr. Serrano was my father and I'm not him."

"What shall I call you then?" she asks, a light tone in her voice.

"Hanson is fine," I say.

"Alright," she says. "Hanson."

A shiver tickles the hair on the back of my neck.

"What shall I call you?" I quip. "Miss James?"

Please say no. Please say no. Please say no.

"You can call me Thea," she says.

"Okay," I say. "Thea." I watch the muscles in her throat carefully swallow as her name rolls off my tongue and I take that as a good sign. "I brought you something."

"What?" she says, her eyes darting from side to side. "Why?"

"Oh, I'm a bad boy, remember?" I tease. "I have to charm your pants off."

"Oh my god," she says. "No, I would prefer to keep them on."

Somewhere in my mind, I make a note that I'd like to make her regret those words, but that is a very different, darker part of my brain entirely.

I present the brown paper bag, holding it out to her. But if her body language is saying anything, it's that she definitely thinks there's a bomb or a snake inside.

"I'll hold it," I say. "You just open it."

She looks toward the kids, who've been mostly talking to each other but I guess at the mention of a surprise, their interest piqued. They definitely look more excited than she does.

There's a heavy reluctance in her movements as she takes half a step forward to close the distance. Her hands reach for the folded over top and begin to pull it open. All I can do is hold my breath while I wait to see if this works or not.

Her eyes scan the contents of the bag over and over again. They dart back and forth and I get the impression her mind is trying to solve the riddle.

All at once, she begins laughing. Not a small, courtesy laugh. A real, deep belly laugh. And it's beautiful to behold.

"You're an idiot," she says between giggles as she reaches into the bag.

Her hand produces a bag of all-purpose flour. She digs her other hand in and pulls out the almond flour. Handing both to the kids for a moment, she then pulls out cake flour and whole wheat flour.

"I don't get it," Ava says.

"Neither do I," Ethan says.

"Guys," Thea says. "He brought me flours. Instead of flowers. Get it? They sound the same but they're spelled differently."

The two children hand the bags of flour back to her as they shrug their shoulders.

"Grown-ups are weird," Ava says. "Ethan and I will be over here when you're ready."

Thea and I give each other a look, knowing full well they'll understand one day.

"This is clever," she says, a smile on her face for the first time in our brief conversations. "But I still can't go out with you."

I hold the bag open as she drops the flours in. "How come?"

"Well, for starters, my date with Clint went pretty well. Remember him? You disapproved based on his name."

"Oh, I remember," I say. "Tell me what you mean by 'went pretty well' then?"

"I mean just that. It was good. Like not perfect, but good," she says, shrugging.

"And you don't think a first date should be perfect?" I ask. "If it's not perfect now at the moment of ignition, it's not going to improve later."

"Perfection is overrated," she says. "I'm planted firmly in reality."

"Then permission to speak freely about reality?" I ask.

Her shoulders relax a bit as she eyes me. "Alright."

"Perfection, for me, is not about being actually perfect. Think of it as an abstract painting. It's not actually perfect by the clinical definition. But as you look at it, you sigh and it is perfect just the way it is." I pause for a moment, letting that sink in. "So when I say a perfect first date should be a requirement for you, I mean, that even with all the tiny imperfections, if you're not dropped off at your front door, the linger of a kiss still on your aching lips, sighing at just how lovely your evening was, then it's less than you deserve."

Her stunned silence lingers for several moments, and I can tell she doesn't know what to say.

"Ava," I call out. "Let's head home, *princesa*."

I sit the bag of flours down as the two children scurry over, Ava taking me by the hand.

"Bye Miss James," she says. "See you tomorrow."

"You have a lovely evening, Thea," I say, smiling.

Turning away from her in the direction of the shop, I'm oddly satisfied with today's progress. Okay, yes, I was rejected for a second time by the same woman in two days. That's not great. But I feel a little give.

It's like when you're opening a pickle jar. At first, it won't budge. Then, there's slight movement. The jar still isn't opening, but you can feel it giving way as if it wants to open but hasn't yet.

And I think Thea James very much wants to open.

## MIND OVER MATTER
### THEA

That son of a bitch. That asshole son of a bitch. Hanson got me good today. I wasn't expecting his wit and this level of charm. But I still won't be fooled. Besides, what the hell am I going to make with all this flour? Of course, I'm thinking all this while trying to mask my smile and make room for the flours in my pantry cabinet.

All that's replayed in my mind since seeing him is the way he says my name. Thea. There's a certain emphasis on the Th sound and then the rest sounds more like an exhale than anything. And it's hot as hell. Why? Why does he also have to have an accent?

"Hey, Mom?" Ethan asks from his place at the kitchen table.

"Yeah, bud?" I push the last bag into place and shut the door, turning toward him.

"Do you think me and Ava could hang out? Like outside of school?" he asks.

My heart does a little flip flop, wondering if this is the moment he goes from being my little boy to being crazy about girls.

"Um, I'm not sure," I say, coming to sit next to him. "What do you want to do?"

"Well, like, she was saying she could help me with my math," he says. "And I mean you're the math teacher and really good, but I was thinking having her help might be better for me."

I get this. I totally get this. Learning from a peer is very different from learning from an adult. And sometimes it's hard being his mother, his teacher, and his tutor all at once.

"Oh, well, I think that would be a great idea," I say. "I don't know if she's going to be available since she's got a lot of stuff going on at home, but I will try to check for you, okay?"

"Okay," he says, seeming satisfied with that answer.

"Hey, bud? Can I ask you a question?" I'm hesitant, but this feels like a good time for it.

"Sure," he says.

"Do you like Ava as just your friend? Or do you maybe like her as more than a friend?" I ask.

"Mom, jeez," he huffs. "She's just my friend. She's cool."

"Okay," I say, holding my hands up in defense. "Okay, I was just asking. Because it would be okay if you did, you know? It's natural and normal."

"Oh my god, Mom, stop," he says. "We are just friends. Please don't be weird."

I back off completely then, leaving him to his snack and

homework. Weird? I'm not weird, am I? I suppose your mom being your teacher can already make it weird with the other kids. But he's clearly not ready to approach the topic of crushes and romantic feelings. God, that sounds weird even in my mind. My son. Romantic feelings.

It's these sort of moments I wish Shane was here. Like, really here. Boys should have a father figure to talk to about this stuff. Of course, I know I'm not the only single mom with a son, and they turn out just fine. I know he's going to be alright. Sometimes I'm just sad for what he's missing out on with a real father figure around.

Shane is what I call a "vacation parent". It's all fun all the time. He doesn't have to worry about homework or bedtimes, doctor's appointments, or scheduling. He doesn't make Ethan do chores or even bathe if he doesn't want to. Luckily, I've instilled in Ethan great hygiene habits that he takes with him when he's there. But Shane is forever the fun parent. Dessert before dinner, staying up late, soda pop, and new toys. All of it. I get stuck with the harder parts. Or actually, all the other parts.

A loud sigh escapes me as I shuffle back to my room for five "me time" minutes before I have to think about starting dinner. Flopping down on the edge of my bed, I slip my shoes off onto the floor and flex my toes as far as they'll go. I could really use a good full-body massage. As you age, things start to ache and you don't even know what the fuck they are. Is it a muscle? A nerve? A bone? Who knows.

Luckily, tomorrow is an easy school day. We have a math

test, and the rest of the period is free time. I always allow free time on test days. Their brains need a little break.

Plus, it gives me time to grade the tests so I don't have to take them home with me over the weekend. And considering I have a second date with Clint, that would be great.

Oh shit, that reminds me! He texted me earlier and I didn't have a chance to reply. I pull my phone out to see what he said.

**CLINT: How does an art show downtown sound? Then dinner at my place?**

Oh god. My stomach does a weird thing and for a moment I think I might vomit my gallbladder or some other internal organ. Dinner at his place. It may seem casual to some but for me, it feels both too soon and also there's a bed at his place. Dinner at someone's home always means they're wanting to get more physical. Right? At least that's my experience.

My fingers hover over the keyboard for a moment as I contemplate my response. On the one hand, I do want another date with him. I think. But I don't think I want to put myself in a situation where something physical is a possibility. Especially not on a second date with someone that I'm only lukewarm about.

**ME: The art show sounds great, but there's this lovely Thai restaurant right downtown near the art district that I've been dying to try. Could we go there?**

**CLINT: Oh sure, that's fine too. Send me the details and I'll make a reservation.**

Breathing a sigh of relief, I type out the information for the place and lay my phone down. You can't really discern someone's emotions from a text but he seems to be fine with it. We haven't even had a first kiss, so I don't want to go straight from where we are to such an intimate setting.

I mean, he kissed me on the cheek at my door at the end of our first date, but that's it. Which was fine with me. In fact, I'm not even sure how I'd have felt if he went for an actual kiss. I guess in addition to wanting to date someone completely opposite of my usual type, I also want to take it glacial slow. While simultaneously feeling like a strong wind could get me off. Super.

I move from my bed back to the pantry to grab the ingredients for dinner and catch sight of the flours once again. It's hard to miss them, considering. Of course, this sends my mind into a Hanson tailspin. Questions begin to bombard me. Like, is he bringing something for me again tomorrow? Will he give up after today? How long will he be on duty as the person who picks up and drops off Ava? Is he the person I should ask about Ava and Ethan hanging out or should I text Drew? Has he ever tattooed himself? What tattoos are hidden behind his clothing? This is the disturbing loop that plays as I chop broccoli and throw it in the pan.

I should not be thinking about any part of Hanson that's covered by clothing. Not even his fucking feet. Basically, if I can't see it when he's picking up Ava, it's none of my business. But god, I bet it's nice. Oh my god, stop.

I throw myself into dinner, chopping carrots and mushrooms to add to the pan, then start on the chicken breasts. Ethan and I eat a lot of stir-fries and teriyaki. He loves them and it's a guaranteed way to make sure he's eating vegetables. I can't complain.

We have a routine down. I make dinner and he sets the table after he's done with his homework. Then I serve food as he grabs us something to drink from the fridge. It's been just the two of us for so long, my other concern with dating is finding someone who won't interrupt our flow too badly. Rather, we need someone who fits in with us.

Staring across from Ethan as he takes his first bite, I'm overwhelmed with my love for him. All I know is, no matter what happens, we are going to be just fine.

## IDK YOU YET

### HANSON

The shop is quiet this morning when I arrive early to pick up Ava. I've never been one to show up before it's open, so seeing it in the early morning sunrise is quite different. The shop windows are east facing and so, it's spectacular actually. It sort of makes me wish I'd arrived earlier before now.

The back door opens behind me, but I don't move from my spot. Even with my back to it, I know it's Will bringing Ava down to me. I can't explain how I know, how I can sense it, but I can.

"Good morning, Hanson," Ava says, running up to my side and grabbing my hand. "What are you looking at?"

"Good morning, *princesa*," I say. "The sunrise." I point into the yellow gold beams rising over the buildings across the street. Orange hues are melting into subtle pinks and if I know anything, it's that this place has some of the best sunrises I've ever seen.

"Oh," she says. "It's very pretty."

"*É o que?*" I ask.

Ava is silent for a moment, searching for the right words. I know she knows them but I don't push.

"*É muito bonito,*" she says.

"*Perfeito,*" I say. "Ready to go?"

Ava nods, adjusting the straps on her backpack, and then we're out the door. Despite being a little older, she still always holds my hand as we walk. Not that I'm complaining. It's quite the opposite. I very much enjoy these moments, as they've existed outside of these mornings too.

"Can I ask you a question?" she asks.

"*Sim*, of course," I say.

"Are you trying to make Miss James your girlfriend?" she asks.

Wow. Walked right into that one, didn't I? I should know by now that Ava is much smarter and much more observant than any of us give her credit for. Then again, it's not like I've been subtle about my advances.

"Well," I say, scratching the back of my neck with my free hand. "It's not as simple as that when you're an adult. I know in school, two kids like each other, and they're instantly matched. But as an adult, there's a little more to the process."

"Well, what's the process?" she asks.

I hesitate, wondering just how much of this I should be sharing or if this is a conversation her mother or Hawk should be having with her. But we've always been pretty open around the shop and with her, so I don't think I'm in danger of over-sharing.

"When you're older and you are interested in someone beyond friendship, you ask them out on a date. This doesn't mean they're automatically your girlfriend. You use some dates to get to know each other. You see if your personalities match and make sure there's chemistry between you."

"What's chemistry? That's not a class?" she asks.

"It's a class, but it's also used as a term to describe if two people mesh well, like if they connect. Does that make sense?"

"I think so," she says. "So, you're trying to see if you and Miss James have chemistry and then if you do, you would make her your girlfriend?"

"Maybe," I say. "She has a decision too."

"Hmm," she says. "I mean, it would be cool if you and Miss James were together and I could see Ethan outside of school. But I wouldn't want you to break up so maybe it's not a good idea."

We cross an intersection, my brows furrowing in confusion at her statement. "Why do you think we'd break up?"

"Because you break up with everyone, Hanson," she says. "You're kind of a heartbreaker."

Ava's words hit me hard, right in the gut. I'm a heartbreaker? Me? That can't be right. Is that how everyone sees me? Shit, if Ava is saying it, then everyone else definitely thinks it. God. When did that become who I am?

We walk the rest of the way to her school in silence. In my mind, I'm going through the Rolodex of girlfriends I've had, each situation, and who broke up with who. I grow more concerned with each encounter, as I begin to notice a distinct pattern, resulting in me always doing the breaking up. And I instantly hate everything.

"Goodbye, Hanson," Ava says as she walks into the building.

For a moment, I didn't even realize we'd made it here. "I'll see you this afternoon, have a good day!" I yell back enthusiastically, hoping it masks my new growing concern.

I'm a heartbreaker. Me. Hanson Serrano. Fuck. This is alarming news to me. I never took myself for any type of player or the one who does the breaking. Perhaps it's been more of an under-the-radar pattern. Well, under the radar to me but glaringly obvious to Ava. Yeah, that doesn't seem right. I'm going to have to do some investigating.

On my way back to the shop, I grab two coffees and breakfast sandwiches for myself and Jericho. We'll be the only ones here for several hours and it's an unusually quiet day, with no appointments until much later. I suppose we could get a random walk-in or two, but even then they're usually quick.

"Hey, man," I say, walking inside as the bell overhead chimes.

"Do I see coffee in your hands from that shop on the corner?" he asks.

"Lady Coffee Bean," I say. "That's the name of the place. And, yes, you do. Plus two of her finest fat stacked breakfast sandwiches."

"Oh my god, yes," he says. "I'm starving."

Jericho unwraps the sandwich at lightning speed and wastes no time taking a huge bite. He wasn't kidding about being hungry.

"Let me ask you a question, man," I say.

"What's up?" he says.

"Do you think I'm a player?" I ask, taking a bite from my sandwich.

Jericho wipes his mouth on the back of his hand and laughs a bit. "No way."

"Are you sure?" I ask.

"Yeah, dude," he says. "Very sure."

"Okay, well, am I a heartbreaker?" I sip from my coffee.

Jericho starts to shake his head, then pauses. "Hmm, well, my first instinct was to say no again but upon a closer look, you do seem to do most of the breaking up."

"But it's not like I want to," I say. "It's just not working out."

"But it seems to not work out for you a lot, and only on your end. Based on what I've seen and when we've talked, the woman is usually all in. Then suddenly, you're out."

Sitting back in my seat, I'm a bit shaken by this response. Over the years, I have been the one to end the relationships. I mean, I haven't had one in a while, but back when I was actively dating, I did end it more often than not. And yes, some of those women did think we were in a way different place than I thought.

For them, things were getting really serious. For me, not so much. It didn't seem fair to lead them on.

"Listen, man," Jericho says. "I don't think you did it on purpose. Hell, I don't even think you enjoyed it. That's the difference. Okay, so you've broken some hearts. But that doesn't make you a heartbreaker. Know what I mean?"

I turn his words over in my head for a moment and to my surprise, they make me feel better. He's right. I didn't enjoy it.

"You're right, man," I say. "Thanks."

Jericho nods as we finish the rest of our sandwiches and coffee in silence. I make plans to run a couple of errands at lunch, including stopping to get what's needed for today's attempt at wooing Thea James. If she thought she could dissuade me after one day, she's got a surprise in store. And let's be clear. This isn't a normal thing for me. I don't exactly spend a lot of time trying to convince a woman to give me a chance. But my gut tells me she does want to, and for whatever reason, is resisting. If I thought for a second she genuinely wasn't interested, I wouldn't be doing this.

She said men bring flowers, chocolate, and teddy bears. And that's exactly what I plan to do.

## SHAKE THE ROOM

### THEA

I wish I could say I was surprised to see Hanson waiting outside for Ava, another brown paper bag in his hand. But I'm not. I don't think my laughing and agreeableness yesterday helped in halting his efforts.

Ethan and Ava run toward him as I trail behind, making every attempt to hold a poker face.

"*Olá*, Miss James," he says.

"Hanson," I say. "To what do I owe the pleasure today?"

"I brought you chocolate," he says. "You know, just checking that list of pebbles off as I go."

"Pebbles?" I ask, confused.

"Like penguins. The males gather pretty stones and leave them at the females' feet for courting. Men do the same. With flowers and chocolates and teddy bears, according to you."

"Ah, right," I laugh. "Penguins."

Hanson nods proudly, adjusting the bag beneath his arm.

"Very well then," I say. "Let's see this latest pebble."

He hands the bag off to me, and I make a note that it's not nearly as heavy as the bag of flours, thankfully. Pulling it open, I immediately recognize the contents. It's a sack full of giant size candy bars. All the good ones. The kind with nuts and nougat and peanut butter. Did I mention they're giant? Like literally fucking huge.

"Gourmet chocolate is fine and all," Hanson says. "But we all know none of it compares to a good old-fashioned peanut butter cup."

He's right, of course. I don't know who decided gourmet chocolates in those heart-shaped boxes had to be filled with weird orange cream and gritty coconut crap, but anytime I've ever been gifted one, I never finish it.

"Thank you," I say. "I agree too. These are better."

"I'm glad you like them," he says. "Despite the cleverness of flours, this one feels more useful."

"I agree," I say. "But it doesn't land you a date."

"Why would it?" he asks. "We've got one more pebble to collect."

"Mom?" Ethan's voice cuts in.

"Yeah, what's up?" I ask, taking this opportunity to direct my attention away from that smile Hanson is flashing at me.

"Ava said she can help me," he says. "She can tutor me."

"Oh right, I'd forgotten," I say. "Um, let me ask Hanson. You all go play over there."

The pair of them walk off in the direction I pointed, leaving me again alone with Hanson.

"So, I know you guys have a lot going on over there, but Ethan is struggling in math, and even though his mother is the math teacher, he seems to think having a peer to help him may be beneficial. He and Ava get along so well and she's top of the class, so he asked for her, but-"

"Ava can help him," Hanson says, cutting me off. "It's no problem. I can help with logistics."

"Are you sure?" I ask.

"*Sim*, of course," he says. "Would you like her to come to your house or him to come over or what?"

"Um, well," I say. "I hadn't thought that far ahead, admittedly."

I scan through the calendar in my mind, trying to find a block of time where it would work.

"Could she be free this Saturday?" I ask. "Ethan goes to his father's right at dinner time but we're free earlier in the day."

"Okay, where?" he asks.

The thought of having him bring her to my house unnerves me. He'd know where I live. And he'd be in my apartment. And he'd take full fucking advantage of the situation. Well, no. I don't mean he'd make a physical move. But we'd be closed in, and he'd be able to try to persuade me to go on a date and I would have no escape. Eventually, I would break down and we'd have a wonderful time. Then we'd probably fuck against the back of my front door as soon as I invited him in for a nightcap. And then, in two weeks, I'd be pouring wine into my ice cream and spooning the mixture straight from the carton to my mouth. Wow, exaggerate much? Get a grip.

"How about a picnic at the park?" I blurt out. "I'll bring it. It's the least I can do for her help."

"Sure, do you want to give me your number so we can coordinate the specifics the day of?" he asks.

NO, I DON'T WANT TO GIVE YOU MY NUMBER. ALERT. ABORT. "Um, I don't know. What if you take advantage of having it and berate me for a date at all hours of the day and night?"

Hanson laughs. "I pinky promise no such thing will happen. Unless it's about Ava and Ethan meeting up, I promise not to use it at all. If I do, you can block me."

He draws a little X over his heart with his index finger, but that doesn't stop my eyes from squinting apprehensively.

"Fine," I say. "Give me your phone."

Hanson happily hands it over and I know he thinks he's one step closer to closing the deal. I punch my number into his phone and text myself from it.

"There," I say.

"Great," he says. "I'll see you tomorrow."

"Yes, I'm sure you will," I say, unable to stop my smile this time.

Ava runs over to him as he waves for her, and I watch the pair walk off in the direction of the studio. I know exactly where it is. I've never been there personally, but I know the place. It's a very successful shop.

"Ethan, honey, let's get going," I call out.

My mind begins the tedious job of sorting through all my racing thoughts as it attempts to prioritize them so I know what the hell I'm doing next. It's always like this. The school day ends, but nothing is over.

Before we can land home, we have to go to the grocery

store, the pharmacy, and the shoe store because Ethan says his shoes "fit but aren't comfortable". Although, he can't tell me what that means. I asked him if something is rubbing against his foot, if there's a lump or something in the sole, or if we're lacing them too tight, but to all those, his answer is no. This leaves him shrugging and I am confused as hell. So, we're off to the shoe store.

Of course, I know that tomorrow Hanson will be bringing me another pebble, the next day I'll be meeting with him off school grounds for a longer period than these afternoon encounters, and then I have a date that night with Clint that may turn out to be more than my tired brain can process.

I'll hand it to him, Hanson certainly does leave an impression. Between his devilish good looks, his charming wit, and sheer persistence, it's proven difficult to remain true to my newfound path to a better romantic relationship.

And by better, I mean good for me. And by good for me, I mean... fuck it, let's call it what it is. It's been boring. But maybe it just starts boring and gets better? That doesn't seem right. Ugh. Life is dumb. Love is dumb.

"Hey, Mom," Ethan says, interrupting my thoughts at the right moment for a second time today.

"Yes, honey?" I ask.

"Can we get pizza for dinner?" he asks.

Normally, I would object. I tend to try to keep our pizza outings to the weekends because it's also when I let him have soda. But with the help of a mess I need to sort out in my mind, not cooking sounds like a pretty good fucking plan.

"Sure," I say. I add stopping to get pizza to my mental

checklist, which also means I can remove going to the grocery because dinner tonight is why I was going.

"Hey, Mom?" Ethan says again.

"Yes?" I ask. We're in the car now, exiting the parking lot, which will be gridlocked for another twenty minutes.

"Do you like Hanson?" he asks.

Oh dear god. "Why are you asking that?"

"Ava says he likes you so I was just wondering," he says.

"She said that, huh?" I turn out of the lot toward the pharmacy.

"Yeah," he says. "Ava says he must like you."

"How does she know that?" I swear children know too much. They hear too much. If you ever need dirt, ask whatever kid has been standing around. They will know something.

"She said his eyes glow when he sees you," Ethan says, spilling these truths as he mindlessly stares out the window at passing buildings.

"Interesting," I say, making a mental note.

"So do you like him back?" he asks.

"Why do you ask? Would that bother you?" I ask. It's not even about liking Hanson or not. But I'm mindful of how my relationships and dating affect Ethan. I'm much more aware of it than his father. Shane's introduced them to probably no less than ten or twelve women over the years, swearing each time that "it's serious". But he's never right about that. Ever.

"I'm just asking because your eyes glow too," he says.

Fuck, fuck, fuckity, fuck. Note to self, make eyes less glowy.

"And no, it wouldn't bother me," he says. "You're my mom, you deserve to be happy."

An invisible claw reaches into my chest and squeezes my heart so hard it might burst. Ugh. Kids are so much smarter than we give them credit for. My son, my baby boy, just wants me to be happy.

And I owe it to him to try.

## POINT OF NO RETURN
### HANSON

We're only a week into this arrangement and I've already grown so fond of it, I hope it lasts a while longer. Sure, I hate the circumstances that created this opportunity, but it doesn't mean I can't enjoy the silver linings.

And yeah, I'm talking about Thea James, sure. But I'm also talking about the one-on-one time I'm getting with Jericho at the shop, and the extra time with Ava. She doesn't know it, but her presence brought a much-needed light into the shop. We were all just sort of out there, free-floating, not knowing what the hell we were doing. Drew and Ava's arrival had a domino effect. A wonderful one to boot.

"Are you leaving to get Ava soon?" Will asks.

In fact, she asks me every day at roughly the same time.

"Yes, in about ten minutes," I say. Which is what I say every single day in return. Because that's when I've been planning to leave all day.

"Okay, just making sure," she says. "How's that going?"

"It's good," I say. "I'm enjoying it."

"No, I mean the part about crushing on her teacher?" She laughs.

"Oh," I laugh. "It's good. I'm enjoying it."

She rolls her eyes at my shenanigans. "Make any headway or are you just pestering the poor woman to death?"

"I want to say I'm making headway, but it's too early to tell," I reply.

"Well, I, for one, am looking forward to the weekend," she says. "Having Knox has been fun, but Auntie Willette needs a break."

"Oh, do Hawk and Drew not need help over the weekend?" I ask, realizing I need to solidify the picnic somewhere in here.

"They say they've got it," she shrugs.

"Nonsense, there's no way," I say.

"That's what I said," she says.

"Well, I'm supposed to take Ava to meet Ethan and her teacher at the park on Saturday. Ethan wants her to tutor him," I blurt out. "Do you think that will be okay with them?"

"Oh, so we are making headway," Will says, a wry smile spreading over her mouth as her arms cross over her chest.

"Trust me, I wish. It's not like I came up with the idea," I say.

"Still, it's more time to pester," she says, walking closer toward me. "I think you got it in the bag."

She smacks me on the arm a couple of times before disappearing into the office down the hallway.

"I think she's right," Jericho chimes in from over his booth wall.

He hasn't spoken a word this entire time and just spouts off with that before he's right back to quiet as a church mouse. The only sound is the hum of his tattoo gun against his client's skin who, thankfully, is wearing headphones. I'm always delighted when clients do that. I don't have to put a lid on myself quite as much.

Maybe they're right. Maybe one or two strategic moves from now, Thea and I will be sitting down to dinner and laughing and I'll try to see if I can make her blush. But if life's taught me anything at all, it's don't make assumptions and don't count on anything being predictable.

There's a fine line with Miss Thea James I have to tread. During their mating season, male Tasmanian devils have to beat the female into submission. If he's too timid, she will beat him up. Of course, we aren't Tasmanian devils. But something can be said about effort. No, I'm not going to roundhouse kick her or anything, but it's still about effort. The female Tasmanian devil wants a fight and you must give her a fight. Thea James wants consistent effort and reliability. If you don't give the devil her smacks, she smacks you back. If I don't give Thea her stability, she'll end up having unfulfilling sex while screaming the name "Clint" and I don't care what you say, that's not a name anyone wants to scream. It sounds like clit. You know it, I know it, even Clint knows it.

Checking the clock after my internal monologue about Tasmanian devil fight club sex and my arch-nemesis—a mystery man named Clint—I realize it's time to head out to get Ava. I reach for the last pebble—the final brown paper bag—next to my workstation and make my way out the door. There's little wiggle room for creativity with teddy bears, so really it just comes down to the one I've chosen. I made a serious effort to find one she's hopefully never seen and will never expect. But that's all I can do.

The fate of what could be between me and Thea James rests in the hands of this goddamn teddy bear.

# MANIFEST

## THEA

For the last ten minutes, I've been ferociously watching the clock on the wall. Which means I've been mad at myself for approximately nine minutes and fifty-three seconds. Why am I watching the time? Because it's almost the end of the day on Friday and school is letting out in four more minutes? Yeah, sure. But also, I know Hanson is going to be out there with my last paper bag, er, pebble.

Of course, I'm still deep in my belief of rejecting him. I think he knows that. But it's nice to be noticed and—dare I say—pursued with such…vigor. A chill runs down my spine when the word "vigor" crosses my mind. Something about that word feels slightly sexual in nature.

The bell sounds, snapping me from my indecent thoughts, and the next thing I hear is a mess of backpacks being slung over shoulders, chair legs squealing against the floor, and this magical thing that happens as soon as the end of the day arrives—all the children's voices raise one hundred million decibels all at once like someone flipped a switch in the backs of their necks from normal to insane.

"Ready to go, Mom?" Ethan asks from the classroom doorway. He has History class down the hallway for his last period and stops most days so we can walk out together, especially on Fridays.

"Yeah, one second, let me grab my bag. Do you have your homework?" I ask. I got into the habit of asking this given there's been more than a few occasions where I've had to use my work email to ask his other teachers for his assignments on a Sunday night because that's when he conveniently remembered he had homework and forgot it on his desk.

"Yes," he says. "You know, I haven't forgotten my homework in almost a month. You don't have to ask anymore."

"You only remember because I ask you every day," I laugh.

"Hey, Ethan," Ava says, her sweet little voice sounding as she appears in my doorway.

"Hey," Ethan says. "Ready to tutor me tomorrow?"

I'm glad he's got a good attitude about needing a tutor. He could be annoyed by the whole thing, and hate the process, but his demeanor has been so calm and accepting.

"Yeah," she says. "I'll have you mathing circles around our class in no time."

On the one hand, it's hard for me to see Ethan doing that, but on the other I know if anyone can get him to, it's Ava. I'm excited to see the results of this little experiment. I know they say you shouldn't do experiments on kids, but this one is interesting. I've been trying to come up with a topic for my Master's Degree thesis and peer-based tutoring or learning versus student to teacher or authority figure is quite the interesting comparison. Nothing is saying I can't get my son help in math and also use it for self-gain, right?

"Let's go," I say. "Ava, is your uncle coming to get you again today?" I try hard to make that sound casual as if it's just simple curiosity. Though, I think they both know my real motive.

"Yes," she says, beaming up at me with the cheesiest grin on her face.

"Don't do that," I say, attempting to mask my own emotions.

"Do what?" Ethan asks, a matching grin all over his face. I swear the only time that boy looks like his father is when he's being a little turd.

I give them both the stink eye before we exit the building. My eyes travel to the right, directly to the spot where I know Hanson will be standing. And he doesn't disappoint. There he is, a paper bag tucked under his left arm and his fingers inside his pocket. Vigor.

Pushing my shoulders back, the kids and I make our way over to him as he stands from his leaning position against the post behind him.

"Hello, there," I say.

"Hi," he says, smiling.

Ava clears her throat from between us.

"Ah, *olá, princesa*," he says, his free arm coming around her shoulder.

"*Olá*, Hanson," she says.

"Hello," Ethan says.

It's a myriad of greetings as everyone takes turns and then silence falls over the four of us. I look down at the two beaming faces between me and Hanson. The children seem to be enjoying this.

"How about you-" I start.

"We know, we know," Ethan says. "We'll be over here when you're done."

I shake my head, laughing a little at the fact that even they know the routine at this point.

"How are you today?" Hanson asks.

"I'm alright," I say. "It's Friday, and that always makes me happy."

"I bet," he says. "Only one kid for the next two days."

"He's going to his dad's after our park trip tomorrow and I'm not getting him back until he comes to school Monday morning," I say. I don't know why I said that. What does it matter?

His eyebrows perk up just a tad as he and I both realize that I've divulged I will be alone for some time.

"So," I say, changing the subject. "What's in the bag?" As if I don't already know. Although, he didn't exactly take my list at face value, so I'm sure there's some sort of odd twist awaiting me inside.

"Here," he says.

I take the bag from him, noting how light it is in comparison to the others. Opening it slowly, I reach inside. My fingers meet soft fluffy material and I tug it out to reveal what —at first glance—is a teddy bear holding a heart-shaped pillow thing. Until I read it.

"SHIT BITCH U IS FINE" is scrawled across the red fabric of the heart in bold capital letters and I lose all control.

My laugh turns from a reserved behind the hand giggle to an all-out cackle loud enough to turn heads, so I do my best to keep the message hidden from onlookers. Hanson is laughing with me, only not so much for the same reason. My guess is he's pleased with my reaction to the bear, please with himself. And he should be, honestly. That was certainly unexpected.

I compose myself after several more minutes and resolve to give him his due praise.

"You did good on that one," I say. "I'll give you that much."

"Thanks," he says. "I tried."

There's silence again, though it's not heavy. Somehow the words stretch between us without actually being said.

*I still can't go on a date with you.*

*Yeah, I know, but it was worth a try.*

Not knowing what else to do, I shift the conversation to safer grounds. "So, I'll see you at the park tomorrow?"

"Yeah, of course," he says.

"Great, I'll text you later with an exact time," I say.

"*Vou esperar por isso, deusa,*" he says.

"What's that mean?" I ask.

He smiles to himself. "Ava, let's go," he calls. "Maybe I'll tell you one day."

If I could remember at all what any of the words that fell from his mouth were, I'd try to spell them into Google translate, but I'll be the first to admit the only thing I could focus on was the way his mouth made the words, the shape of his lips making the vowels. I don't even know which vowels they were. Ugh. Accents. Ugh. Boys who can speak other languages. It's not fair. It's like a secret weapon.

I think back on my brief history of dating and realize not a single one was bilingual. They've all been white. Granted, most of the brief history is Shane. I don't think it was ever on purpose. I know it wasn't. Because Hanson has to be one of the most attractive men I've ever had the pleasure of meeting in person. And yet, here I am, rejecting him. When I frame it that way, it doesn't sound smart at all.

"Mom," Ethan's voice pulls me from my thoughts.

"Yeah, honey?" I ask.

"Are you okay? You've been staring at Hanson walking away for a while," he says.

Oh my god. "Yeah, I'm fine, let's head home."

With my teddy bear hugged to my chest, we make our way to the car, and eventually out of the parking lot. All the while, I contemplate back and forth, teetering on a mountain of indecisiveness. A few days ago, I was hard set against giving Hanson a chance. In fact, despite his good looks, I allowed myself zero butterflies. But now… a long sigh escapes me as we arrive home. I don't even know how we got here. It's like I was on auto-pilot the whole way.

Let's be rational for a minute. I know Hanson's hot. Fine. But it's not like I know for sure I'm missing out on something more than surface good looks and likely a pretty good sense of humor, based on his pebbles. He could still be a jerk. Though, based on his relationship with Ava, that's doubtful. Fine. He's a nice, good-looking guy, with a great sense of humor, and clearly, he's good with children. But he could still be a man slut. Or bad in bed. Or financially irresponsible. Wow, that's a lot of maybes.

---

After dinner, Ethan and I do our evening routine. He showers and I pack his bag for Shane's house. We read and I tuck him into bed. Once the dishes are done and the house is put away for the night, I change into pajamas and pour myself a glass of wine—my favorite red blend—and resolve to curl up in front of the television for a little while before bed.

It's on these rare occasions that I finally feel a slight weight lifted from my shoulders. Sometimes doing this whole single mom thing feels like an endless number of fires to put out, things to be done, and dinners to make. You have to find moments, and steal away twenty minutes here and there to feel separate from the label that seems to become your whole identity. Sometimes I don't feel like Thea anymore. Just Mom, Ethan's mother.

I swear I was an entire person before the moment he was born. But sometimes it's hard to see her.

I absentmindedly reach for the bear Hanson gave me, which I placed on the couch when I sat my bags down earlier.

I read the words again as I take another large gulp of my wine and smile. The next thing I know, I'm reaching for my phone.

*Just tell him what time tomorrow. Just tell him what time tomorrow. Just tell him what time tomorrow.*

**ME: I have a question.**

## ALMOST (SWEET MUSIC)
### HANSON

Every evening before I sit down to relax, I do two things. I do them every day, and I do them without fail. First, I take a trip downstairs to the basement of my building to use the exercise room. Even if all I have left in me for the day is twenty minutes of cardio, I do it. For me, exercising isn't even about looking good. It's about the release of anxiety and other negative emotions pent up inside. Exercise as a means to improve your mental health isn't for everyone, and I'm not one of those assholes that swear you'll be happy if you just smile and lift weights. But I do find that it works for me.

This evening, I seem to have a touch more energy than expected and blow through my chest and arms routine pretty damn fast. So, I turn to the treadmill for a quick ten-minute cool-down session.

Most people prefer to put some headphones on and listen to music while they exercise. They rely on the energy of the music to flow through them and keep them motivated. I, on the other hand, listen to documentaries and podcasts. It could be anything from an in-depth look at what goes on in the stock market to the latest theory about the Zodiac Killer to the migration patterns of birds.

I don't know why I'm like this. No one understands and sometimes they even assume I hate music, which I promptly set the record straight on. I just like knowledge. I like learning things. When I came to America as a teenager, I used documentaries to better learn English. I spoke some English, but I attribute my fluency to listening to these things.

Just as I'm about to hear a woman deconstruct the female orgasm, my phone buzzes from its place on the treadmill. The screen lights up, showing a text so I grab it and instantly smile. Thea James has a question.

ME: What's that?
THEA: Why?
ME: Why what?
THEA: Why me?
ME: Why not you?
THEA: Do you answer all questions with another question?

I laugh as I power down the treadmill and step off, running my hand over the fly-away hairs that fell from my hair tie.

ME: To be fair, the first question was warranted.
THEA: And the second?
ME: It seemed obvious.
THEA: Well it's not.

I take a moment as I step into the elevator and press the

button for the second floor. The very idea Thea needs to ask why as if she can't understand why or see her value makes me a little sad.

Climbing out of the elevator a few moments later, I reply just before walking into my apartment.

**ME: Who made you feel like you need to ask why?**

The text bubble appears, then disappears, reappears again, and disappears again before I get an answer.

**THEA: There's a strong argument for my son's father.**

I figured that was the case. I hate that for her and all women. Sometimes I meet women who remind me so much of my mother that I begin to wonder if this isn't just a universal epidemic.

**ME: You have worth that extends beyond what I see, or what your ex saw. The question, goddess, is not why we'd be interested in you, but why you'd allow us a seat at your table.**

**THEA: Did you just call me goddess??**

**ME: Yes.**

I slip my workout clothes off, throwing them into the hamper as I reach into the shower to turn on the water.

**THEA: No one has ever called me that before.**

**ME: I'm sorry they didn't see your magic.**

**THEA: Stop that.**

**ME: Stop what?**

There's a ledge on the back wall of my shower where I always place my phone. Usually, I leave it there as I wash my hair and body. At the moment, I'm still hovering at the ledge, answering her messages instead as water barely hits my backside.

**THEA:** Saying the nice things

**ME:** Are you drinking?

**THEA:** Are you a wizard?

**ME:** So that's a yes

**THEA:** What are you doing?

**ME:** Showering

I step back into the water while her text bubble does the hide-and-seek dance it did earlier. The warm water does wonders for my upper back muscles as I start to feel the sting of the way I worked them over earlier.

**THEA:** You're impossible

That's all she says, and I take it as a good sign that the mere mention of my showering makes her upset. Mating is a game of strategy. People call it dating or courting, or several other things. But when you break it down to a science, all of the animal kingdoms, humans included, are subject to mating rituals. We just happen to be more complex, and therefore, get to apply complex strategies.

**ME:** I know many who would agree with you

**THEA:** Can you do 11 am tomorrow? At the park?

I reach for a towel, draping it around my hips, and weigh my options but ultimately decide it's too soon for a bold move.

**ME:** Yes, that works. Do I need to bring anything?

**THEA:** If you could just make sure Ava brings her math book and some paper and a pencil, that would be great.

ME: I can do that.
THEA: Thank you.

Hesitation tingles on my fingertips but I still write it.

ME: Is there anything I can help you with tonight?

For a minute, there's no text bubble at all. Then, the familiar whack-a-mole dance as I comb my hair out of my face, then socks from my drawer. I hate being barefoot, which is strange considering we were at the beaches a lot when I lived in Brazil. My mother and I spent many barefoot afternoons in the garden, as well, collecting bugs and rocks and tending to her flowers. Now, though, I can hardly stand it.

THEA: What do you mean by that?

She's baiting. Then again so am I. The question is, which one of us will play the game longer.

ME: I mean exactly what I said, Goddess. Can I help you tonight?

THEA: Help me what??

ME: Whatever you need.

I slide my boxer briefs up over my hips and use the towel to dry my hair. I wait twenty seconds, then thirty. I continue to dry my hair and wait. Sixty seconds go by and still nothing. Walking into the bathroom, I wonder if I've scared her off. Maybe she won't be responding at all. It's been a full five minutes, and still nothing. I brush and floss, rinse, and walk into my room. I've given up hope after ten minutes or so, and then my phone vibrates just as I'm reaching for my journal.

THEA: I'm good, I'll see you tomorrow at 11. Goodnight!

I check the timestamps between my message and hers,

calculating a fourteen-minute window between the two. Did she just…? No, probably not. I'm likely reading way more into that than I should. But wouldn't it be something if my initial thought was correct? Wouldn't it be something if, to my question, she couldn't resist the urge to touch herself? The thought sends a shockwave down my spine.

Shaking my head to clear my mind, I open my journal to the next blank page. The second thing I do each day, without fail, is reflect on the day in my journal. Doctor's orders. I'm required to write three things: a list of three things for which I'm grateful, a list of three things I cannot change, and a list of three things I want to improve for myself.

Tonight, these three lists are easy. Other nights, I struggle immensely and avoid it until the last possible moment. But still, I write them. It's part of my therapy plan, and Dr. Russell often checks my homework. So, I have to do it. More than that though, even when I don't want to do it, afterward, I feel better. And I think that's the most important part.

Tonight I write *Thea, Thea, Thea. Salvador Serrano. Salvador Serrano. Salvador Serrano. My heart. My mind. My art.*

# HATE ME
## THEA

Get. A. Goddamn. Hold. Of. Yourself. Last night was… okay, you know what, last night was a tragic slip—a momentary loss of self-control. Did I, Thea James, a grown-ass woman, experience a moment of weakness when I closed my eyes and imagined Hanson's voice asking me what he can help me with tonight? Yes, yes, I did. Did I also immediately proceed to slip my hand down my fluffy pajama pants and play naughty DJ on the devil's doorbell? Yes, yes, I also did that.

A hint of pink is still present across my cheeks this morning as I try to focus on applying mascara. But every time I make eye contact with myself, the ball of self-loathing in my stomach grows two sizes. And then I think about giving an encore performance and ding dong ditching Satan one more time before we leave the house.

And let me tell you, doing THAT while thinking about

Hanson right before I see Hanson has got to be the dumbest idea I've ever had.

"Mom!" Ethan's shrill voice bellows from the living room. "Are you ready? We're going to be late!"

He's so dramatic. I wish I could say he gets that from his father, but I know it's me. "I'm coming, son."

I'm going to avoid telling him he's right and we are in fact leaving the house ten minutes later than I wanted to, but I was facing an existential crisis in my mirror. See? Dramatics. That's me.

"It's okay," I say. "We can stay ten minutes later to make up."

"And you got the food?" he asks, ignoring the fact that I have a rather large cooler in one hand as we climb into the car.

"Yes, my love," I say. "We're good to go."

"Okay, I just want to make sure," he says. "I'm nervous."

Oh. He's nervous. This makes me think maybe he does have a little crush on Ava. Or maybe he just doesn't want her to be upset with him or frustrated. Tempted to ask him, I bite my tongue instead, knowing it will only add to his nervousness. All the social aspects of this outing aside, I sincerely hope Ava tutoring him helps.

We arrive at the park exactly on time, and I'm counting it, despite being able to see Ava and Hanson standing near a picnic table already. They're throwing a ball back and forth, and I'm finding it hard to breathe as we approach.

"Let me get that," Hanson says, running toward me and relieving my left arm of the rather heavy cooler.

"Thank you," I say. "I probably packed too much." I let out a small laugh, hoping I can shut off the sudden and recurring thoughts of my digit slip while also keeping an outward calm and collected appearance. Please don't be blushing.

"Hey, Ethan," Ava says. "Ready to be a math wiz?"

Well, she's not lacking confidence, I'll give her that. Ava's face is full of gentle excitement as I watch my son take a seat next to her and pull his notebook from his backpack.

"Let's do this," he says.

Hanson circles around the picnic table towards me, a calm smile playing on his mouth.

"Sleep well, *deusa*?" he asks.

"You're going to have to tell me what that means eventually," I say. "But yes, I did. Um, did you?"

"Not usually," he says. "But that's sort of normal for me."

"I'm sorry to hear that," I say.

"Such is life," he says, shrugging his shoulders. "So, what do we do now?"

He has a point. The kids appear to be diving in hard without us, which leaves Hanson and me standing here awkwardly, doing absolutely nothing.

"Uh, well," I laugh. "I guess we just let them do their thing."

"Good," he says. "Perhaps it's our turn to 'go play over there' as we tell them each day."

"Good point," I say.

We begin to walk toward a nearby tree, but in reality, we're aimless. It sort of feels nice to slow down and not feel like I'm "on" for a moment. If all Hanson and I do is walk around this area in silence for thirty minutes, that's fine by me.

"Tell me something," Hanson says.

"What?" I ask.

"Anything. You pick," he says.

"Oh," I say, not hiding the fact that I'm caught off guard. Glancing over at the kids, I recall a childhood memory. "When I was Ethan's age, I wanted to be a private investigator."

"That's an interesting career choice for an eleven-year-old girl," he says.

"Because all girls want to be fashion icons and social media influencers now?" I tease back.

"Maybe," he says, laughing. "But also, it's usually law enforcement rather than P.I. or something like that."

"I guess you're right," I say. "But I wanted to work for myself."

"Smart girl," he says. "And then you fell in love with math?"

I laugh, letting my fingertips graze the rough tree bark. "Not quite. I didn't decide to become a teacher until I was pregnant with Ethan."

"I suppose investigation work can be a little risky," he says.

"I don't really think that was the reason," I say. "Honestly, I just knew I needed to take on a career path that lent itself to having a child."

"That makes sense too," he says.

"And Shane didn't seem like he was interested in making selfless decisions," I say. "Let's just say I've always been the breadwinner. And baker. And server."

"Yes, I gathered that," he says. "I'm sorry, for what it's worth."

I stop circling the tree to take a long hard look over at Ethan, his head tilted toward Ava as he appears to be listening to her intently. "I'm not."

"What about you?" I ask. "You tell me something."

Hanson tilts his head back and forth as if he's attempting to knock something loose inside.

"I came to America as a teenager and stayed with my aunt on my mother's side, but before that, I don't remember wanting to be anything. Not a teacher or a P.I. or anything else. That's odd, isn't it?" he asks.

Part of me wonders how a kid can go so many years without thinking about their future but maybe it's different in Brazil. Maybe kids aren't encouraged to think about that stuff yet.

"I don't know, maybe it's different in Brazil than here?" I ask.

"Maybe," he says. "It was probably just my mother. She liked to keep me distracted with whimsy."

"That sounds nice, actually," I say. "My parents were very practical. It was all about grades and choices and making the right ones."

We stop near a bench, taking a seat as it faces the kids directly but still gives them plenty of space to work alone. They're cute to watch. Sometimes I think adults forget that kids are wholly individual and complex.

"When did you meet Shane?" Hanson asks.

"Ah, yeah. I was a senior in high school. He was twenty-one and the epitome of everything my parents hated and wanted me to avoid. So, naturally, I fell head over heels," I say.

"That will do it," he says. "There's a reason for that quote about curiosity and how it kills a cat."

"Yes, and I was a very stupid cat," I say.

"But you got something great out of it," he adds.

"This is true," I say. "Sort of makes working to put myself through college while pregnant and supporting me and Shane and Ethan all on my own worth it."

"Your parents didn't help with college?" he asks.

"They cut me off when I wouldn't have an abortion," I say, shrugging.

"Jesus," he says. "That's pretty shitty."

"Yeah," I say. "It was. But we've reconciled mostly. They love Ethan now and treat him well. We're okay, but there are still strained moments. Forgiveness is hard."

"I understand that," he says.

"Jesus, I'm sorry. I don't know why I'm spilling all this out to you," I say. And I honestly don't. I'm just vomiting all this up in his lap. This is stuff I don't talk about even on third or fourth dates.

"It's okay," he laughs. "I don't mind. It happens in my profession."

"With people you're tattooing?" I ask.

"You wouldn't believe what strangers tell the person jabbing them with a needle," he says.

"I can only imagine," I say, laughing. "When did you choose your tattoo artist career?"

"Pretty much as soon as I got to America," he says.

His eyes trail from mine down to where my fingers are absentmindedly picking at a notch in the wooden bench. Someone's carved initials into it, the letters "T.J." in bold capitals.

"Who do you think T.J. is?" he asks.

"Tammy Jo?" I say, laughing.

"Tommy John?" he says. "Or maybe it's the guy and girl? Or two guys? Or two girls?"

"You raise a good point," I say, rubbing my chin. "Maybe it's Tina and Jenny."

"Maybe Tyler and John," he counters.

"I guess we will never know," I say, laughing.

"Maybe that's the beauty of it," he says. "We aren't meant to."

I like that. I don't tell him, but instead, let the silence fall around us. There's something to be said about tolerating someone when it's quiet. A person can jabber on and on about nothing at all, and sometimes that's easier than when there are no words spoken. It's hard to explain. But this silence, here with Hanson, doesn't feel so awful and that's saying something.

Birds chirp overhead, and I take note of the unseasonably warm breeze. This time of year, just before spring is in full force, it tends to be much colder still and rainy most days. For a moment, I catch myself re-thinking my outfit for my date with Clint later. Right. My date with Clint. Honestly, I felt more excited about it earlier in the week when he originally made the plans with me. Now, they're feeling a little deflated.

But I won't let that stop me from going. Clint is a nice man, a good man.

Then again, so is the man sitting on this bench with me.

## BURY ME FACE DOWN
### HANSON

Even in the silence, it's not silent. If I listen closely, we're just in earshot of the kids, who are talking about the current math problem they're on. There's a family a few yards away, the parents sitting on a blanket while their toddler tries chasing his older sibling. And then there's Thea as she breathes deeply in and out and back in again. It's almost rhythmic.

I don't think she can see it—how exquisite she is. Maybe that's my luck in this. Her long red hair is wavy today, a natural tossed-around look. She's only wearing a hint of makeup as far as I can tell, maybe a little mascara and blush. There's nothing on her lips, though, except maybe some lip balm or something that keeps them looking moisturized. I don't know why I'm fixated on that. Perhaps, because they look so goddamn kissable I have to intentionally tell myself not to even try it.

But I think the thing I like most about her is probably the

thing she hates the most, or at least I find this true of most women. But Thea's body is magnificent. I can't vouch for what's underneath the clothing, but I can see the thickness of her thighs through her pants and how they don't gap. I imagine the soft flesh over her hips, how they'd be perfect for grabbing, how the warmth of her full figure would make for perfect cuddling. And fucking. Okay, that was out of turn. Too much. Reel it back.

"Do you think we should eat? Maybe have lunch and check in on them?" Thea's voice cuts through my thoughts, pulling me back to reality. Thankfully. I was starting to go off the rail a little.

"Sounds like a good idea to me," I say, rising from the bench.

Stretching my arms overhead, she starts to walk toward the picnic table, leaving me to trail behind. Not that I'm complaining. I'll be the first to tell anyone I'm an ass man. Yes, I love tits. Yes, I love all the parts of a woman. But the ass is where it's at for me. It's so versatile. You can squeeze it, pat it, rub it, the options are endless. You can even bite it. Maybe use it as a pillow. Ugh. A pillow. My favorite. The point is, I like asses and Thea's ass is chef's kiss perfection.

"Hey, how's it going my little mathletes?" she asks as we approach.

"Mom, I did all five of these problems by myself and Ava says they're right," Ethan says.

"That's amazing," Thea says.

Ava looks at me with her unique pride written on her face and I give her a knowing wink.

"Let's eat, then we can see how much more time we have until we need to go meet your dad," Thea says to Ethan.

She starts pulling various containers from the cooler she brought, sitting them down in the middle of the table. It's more containers than I expected honestly and seems like way more food than is necessary for lunch for the four of us.

"I probably packed too much," she says as if she can read my thoughts. "But I wasn't sure what all you and Ava liked so I wanted you to have options."

"That's sweet of you," I say. "Ava likes most things. And I'm easy."

If I'd blinked at that moment, I'd have missed the way her hand hesitated to put that last container down when I said I'm easy. Luckily for me, I wasn't blinking. Thea goes on—presumably to shake the momentary loss of her unaffected facade—and I let her. But something tells me I've made my way under that pretty skin of hers.

Inside the containers are two different kinds of sandwiches plus vegetarian wraps, potato salad, cut-up vegetables with a side of ranch dressing, fresh fruit, and chocolate chip cookies. Plus, she packed us all individual water bottles with cut-up fruit inside.

"This looks amazing," I say as I put a little of everything on my plate.

Ava mumbles her agreement as she takes a large bite from her chosen sandwich and Ethan nods from behind his as well.

"Thank you," she says. "It's nothing special, but it's a small token of my gratitude."

"Well, consider us properly thanked, even though it's not necessary," I say.

'It is, though," she says. "Just looking over these problems the kids did together, I can tell Ava is making a difference, just after this short session."

"I'm glad," I say.

"Me too," Ethan says. "I was starting to worry about my future college goals."

Thea and I both laugh, knowing full well these sixth-grade math woes wouldn't have kept him from his collegiate aspirations, but I'm impressed with his level of concern as I imagine his mom is too.

"If you want, we can do weekly sessions?" Ava says. "You don't think Mom or Hawk would mind, do you, Hanson?"

Her attention turns from Thea to myself as she asks the question, her eyes bright and confident.

"No, *princesa*," I say. "I can bring you until things settle down at home. Then, I'm sure we can figure out an arrangement after that."

Thea's expression turns to relief as I confirm with Ava. It's not like I expected one session to fix it all. Tutoring tends to be an ongoing thing, and I think in this case it's smart.

"Great," Ethan says. "Because I literally can't do this without her."

The sincerity and seriousness in his tone make me crack a smile. It's cute. And judging by Ava's face, she likes it too.

We finish our meal in quiet conversation, the kids throwing out the occasional question or comment about school and math and the other kids. I do a lot of listening and watch as Thea's face lights up at the sounds of their voices as well. Sometimes, she knows what they're talking about, like when Ava rolled her eyes at the mention of some boy named Joel who's in their class. And sometimes, she's as clueless as I am, like when Ethan remarked about some online game all the kids play together.

Each time I found my eyes roaming to Thea's face, it was as if she could feel me, and would return the look. There's something to be said about silent glances that turn to what I can only call intense eye contact. Each moment is a secret between us that all the world can see, but they aren't looking.

As I help her throw away the trash from lunch and re-pack the remaining food back into its containers, the kids work on some additional math problems. Truth be told, the simple act of cleaning up the meal together feels rather intimate. We move well around one another, not once bumping our hands while reaching for the same thing or any of that. It's a perfectly orchestrated dance, and maybe she can't hear the music yet, but I definitely can.

"Gosh," she says, grabbing my attention. "It's later than I thought."

She's looking at the delicate gold watch on her wrist with a disappointed expression, which I'm going to take as a good sign.

"You guys need to go?" I ask.

"Unfortunately," she says. "I have to meet his dad in less than an hour."

"Right," I say. "Well, at the risk of sounding like a broken record, we could grab dinner later? Or maybe a drink?"

Thea's face doesn't immediately harden at the suggestion, and in fact, there's a whisper of a grin threatening to expose itself if she's not careful.

"I can't," she says. "I'm going on a date with Clint, remember?"

I hold onto the fact that her rejection is based on already having plans versus when she previously rejected me for being me. It's progress, right?

"Oh right," I say. "I'm sure that will be nice." Nice is the nicest word I can muster in this situation.

"Yeah," she says, rather unenthusiastically. "Maybe another time, though."

Be cool, be cool. "Sounds good." Nailed it.

After packing up, Ava and I walk Thea and Ethan to their car to say our goodbyes. The kids high-five each other before Ethan crawls into the backseat as I help put the cooler into the trunk.

"Thank you again," she says. "You know, for taking the time to bring Ava. I'm sure you had better things to do with your weekend."

I narrow my eyes at her as I try to assess if she's being serious or cursory. "This is exactly what I wanted to do today. You may find this hard to believe but Ava's important to me, to all of us at the shop."

"Oh no, I didn't mean it like that. Drew says you're all so wonderful. I just meant like you're a young, single guy, you know? And it's the weekend. Party time," she says, a hint of nervousness in her tone.

"I suppose for some men, it is," I say, shrugging. "I like to have a good time just like anyone else, but I hardly ever do anything I'd label 'partying' unless someone drags me out."

"Interesting," she says.

I don't know if she's saying that because she's surprised or impressed or both. All I know is we're lingering at her car door and no one is saying anything and it feels like that moment on a first date when I don't know if they want me to kiss them or not. But this isn't a date, I remind myself. Honestly, I shouldn't need to. Two kids are staring at us so intently that my skin is burning.

"Well," she says. "Let's talk later about doing this again next week, yeah?"

"Sure, yeah," I say. "Drive safe."

With that, she finally opens her car door and slides in. I shut the door behind her, waving through the window one last time as the engine roars to life. As they back out of the parking spot, Ava walks to my side and she waves at Ethan.

"We have a problem," Ava says.

"What's that, *princesa*?" I ask, looking down at her.

"Our crushes just drove away," she says.

Oh boy.

## 10 THINGS I HATE ABOUT YOU
### THEA

Despite my best efforts to avoid being late for my date with Clint, I am in fact running twenty minutes behind when I hear him knock on my door to pick me up. So, after running to the door to let him inside to wait, I run back to my room to finish my makeup as a myriad of apologies flies out of my mouth. I also need to choose shoes, put my essentials in a smaller purse, and apply a second layer of deodorant because I've officially cut through the first application with my thorough anxiety sweat.

It's not my fault, though. Well, it's not all my fault. We only left the park about ten minutes later than I planned. Ethan and I moved as fast as we could to drop the cooler off and pick up his overnight bag from the house before driving to Shane's place of work to drop him off. And of course, Shane got off work forty-five minutes late so we had to sit in the car and wait for him to finally come out. But I wasted no time arguing with him about it and hauled my ass straight back home to shower.

But here we are. I was in such a hurry, I didn't even shave my legs. Normally, I would before any date after the first one, because you never know what could happen. Plus, Clint already tried to arrange the date to be at his house which would definitely warrant shaving everything. Honestly, though, all the excitement and hope I had for this date has slowly depleted over time since initially making the plans.

"You have a nice place," Clint calls from the living room.

"Oh, thank you," I call back. "We've lived here for several years now and I've done a lot of renovating over that time."

My house is by no means a mansion. I'm a single mother who gets less than regular child support payments coupled with a teacher's salary. It's modest but cozy. Over the years, I found myself getting into DIY projects and thrifting old pieces of furniture to upcycle. I guess I'd call my style eclectic.

When I finally step out of my bedroom, Clint's eyes beam as he greets me with a big smile.

"Sorry I'm running late," I say again.

"It was worth the wait," he says.

Despite how hectic today has been, I do find myself smiling at his compliment. Perhaps I can rally that excitement I had before once again. And if nothing else, it's still a nice time out of the house and kid-free. Honestly, I don't know why I'd started to become so blah about tonight.

As Clint opens his car door for me, I remind myself that this is what I've wanted. A nice, reliable guy. Someone who holds my car door open and keeps his promises. Someone who would be a good role model for Ethan. This is what you wanted, Thea.

On the way to the restaurant, Clint attempts to explain his job in further detail, but honestly, I don't understand any of the words coming out of his mouth. Computational. Marginalization. Harvesting efficiencies. But again, he seems passionate. So I nod and smile and raise my eyebrows at the correct times in an effort to respond politely and not look like a dumbass.

As he talks on, flashes of the conversation I had with Hanson surface and drown Clint out a bit. Again, I'm captured by the way his mouth moves when he's talking. And I have to compare the two men, but if Hanson were saying these same big boring words, I don't think I'd care. I could just stare at his mouth the whole time.

My eyes roam to Clint's mouth. His normal, unspectacular mouth. There's some stubble where a mustache should be, and his lips sort of look a little dry. Neither of which entice a kiss or stir any desire in me. It's unfortunate because I was at least hoping for a heavy make-out session. Though, something tells me I'm just no longer interested in making out with Clint tonight, or any night for that matter.

"We're here," he says, pulling off the road into the parking lot of what I know to be a very nice, very expensive restaurant. "I hope you're hungry. This place is incredible."

I bet it is. "Clint," I say. "I'm so sorry, but I don't think we should continue on this date."

"What? Why?" he asks, just as confused as I am even though I'm the one saying the words.

"Because I just don't think we're meshing well. You're a very nice man, and this is all on me but I don't want to lead you on either." I make every effort to wear a soft, apologetic expression as his hands grip the steering wheel tighter.

"Are you serious right now?" he asks. "You couldn't have told me this three hours ago before I got ready, before I came to get you?"

"I'm so sorry," I say. "Truly, I didn't mean to"

"Stop," he says, cutting me off. "Just save it. You clearly don't know when you're looking a gift horse in the mouth."

"What's that supposed to mean?" I ask.

"Oh please," he says. "You're a single mom, your ex is a deadbeat from what I can discern, and you're a teacher which means you make close to no money. This was practically a charity case for me."

With every word flying from his mouth, my blood boils hotter but I make an effort not to snap back and try using my de-escalation training. "Listen, I think you're being intentionally cruel out of anger so I'm going to ignore what you've said. You don't even have to worry about taking me home."

"Yeah, I wasn't going to. You can walk back as far as I'm concerned," he says as he clicks the button to unlock the doors.

"Well, I wish you the very best," I say, opening the door.

"Whatever," he says. "I could've been out with someone else, one of the other women hitting me up. But no. I chose you and all your baggage. I should've known better."

This time, his words stop me in my tracks, one foot on the pavement outside and the other still inside the car. Turning back to him, I plaster on my best fake smile. "Trust me, with your winning attitude, you'll have no trouble getting a date with exactly the right woman. And when she marries you for your money and cheats on you with a man who treats her well, I want you to think of me." I exit the car before he can say anything in return.

Clint's car reverses from the parking spot so fast that I'm genuinely afraid he's going to hit something. Then, the tires squeal against the pavement as he peels out onto the road, nearly sideswiping a truck.

The lesson here, ladies and gentlemen, is when it's too good to be true, it probably fucking is. What a prick.

After several deep breaths, I've managed to calm the shaking in my hands enough to pull out my cell phone. Now, the problem is who the hell do I call? I moved here when Shane and I were still together forever ago and while I've managed to make a few friends, most of my ride-or-dies live hours away.

I could call Shane. The mere thought makes me want to cry. It's not that he wouldn't come to get me, but he'd bitch at me all the way back to my place and I'm not in the mood for that. Fuck it. I'll just get an Uber.

God, this is sad. It's Saturday night, I'm sitting in the back of a Corolla while my driver Tom plays smooth jazz on the radio and I hate jazz. I could tell him to turn it, but I don't have the energy. I'm on my way back home on the one night I don't have Ethan and I'll probably drink a whole bottle of wine while I watch a rom-com and fall asleep in my bowl of popcorn. That sounds sad as fuck.

There's always the hope that I'm in a rom-com myself and will at any moment stumble into the arms of my white knight. But this isn't exactly the fucking Hallmark channel.

There's only one person to blame for this. Okay, maybe two. Well, one person and myself. Whatever. I whip out my phone in a huff and stab at the buttons.

**ME: Well, I hope you're happy.**

I watch and wait for the text bubble to pop up and I don't have to wait long.

**HANSON: Aww thanks, I hope you're happy too.**

**ME: Don't be a smartass.**

**HANSON: What could I have possibly done now?**

I begin to type, then erase, then type again. Nope, not today. I will not give him that satisfaction.

**ME: I'm just distracted.**

**HANSON: I'm going to need more information than that.**

**ME: I'm not on my date.**

**HANSON: Oh no, did he bail?**

**ME: No, no. I did. You know what, this is too much to type. Are you busy?**

**HANSON: I'm not busy, do you want to call?**

**ME: Not exactly.**

I type out my address and ask him over. He agrees too quickly, though, and it has me questioning myself all over again.

**ME: Great. Can you bring wine?**

It's the least he can do after ruining my night. Because he

did. He ruined it with his charm and his wit and his kindness and his stupidly hot body and lickable face.

**HANSON: Be there in twenty.**

Ugh. I make a note to put on the most unappealing pajamas in my wardrobe and then pray he's not wearing what he was earlier. That man knows his way around torn black jeans and classic white T-shirts.

Now if I can somehow avoid letting him know his way around me, I'll be all set.

## IT WON'T KILL YA

### HANSON

Surprised doesn't even cover what I felt when Thea texted me a few short minutes ago. I suppose the term shocked comes close, but it's still not quite right. It's well into the evening, she's inviting me over to her place, and she wants me to bring wine. I don't want to get my hopes up, but this feels like it could be the opening I've been waiting for.

I knock, then smooth my hair back as if I didn't jump up, change my clothes, go to the store for wine, and then drive over here in record time. Luckily, her place isn't all that far from mine.

The door swings open wide as Thea stands with one hand on her hip. If I'm reading her correctly, she's unamused. Or maybe frustrated.

"You're on time," she says, a hint of surprise in her tone.

"Usually," I say.

"Come on in," she says. "Can you take your shoes off? House rules."

"Sure," I say, slipping off one and then the other. I place them next to the others I see near the door and follow behind her as she heads toward the kitchen.

I like her place. It feels cozy and her style is interesting. My eyes dart from one corner of the open floor plan to another, taking it all in. The far wall in the living room captures most of my attention, as it has two large bookcases and several houseplants. It's always a plus when a person takes an interest in keeping something else alive.

Thea pulls two glasses from a cabinet near the sink and places them on the counter.

"Care to open that and pour?" she asks, handing me the corkscrew.

"My pleasure," I say.

I begin to twist it into the cork, making easy work of the task. She leans far over the counter, watching intently and I can't help but notice her cleavage now on full display. It's not my fault, I swear. It's like, right there.

She breathes in deeply, causing her chest to swell and I'm nearly panting as I try to keep my concentration on this wine.

The cork makes a satisfying popping noise as I free it from the bottle.

"Yay," Thea says as she readies the glasses.

I pour a generous amount into both, and she holds her glass up toward me.

"A toast," she says.

"What are we toasting?" I ask.

"You tell me," she laughs. "Anything."

Rubbing my hand over my jaw, I think for a moment about what would make an appropriate toast. Raising my glass to hers, we lock eyes. "To new beginnings. May the endings hurt like hell so you know you felt something. May the healing be as long as you need. And may the start of each new chapter be beautiful."

"A tattoo artist and a poet," she says as the glass meets her lips.

I sip from my glass, shrugging my shoulders. "Sometimes I get the words right, but I'd hardly call myself a poet."

"Let's sit," she says.

Thea walks past me toward the living room and I'm not sad to trail behind her, shamelessly watching her hips sway from one side to the other.

"You like to read?" I ask as we settle into the couch.

Her eyes dart toward the bookshelves behind her, then she nods.

"I do," she says. "For a long time it was about the only entertainment I could afford."

"Fair enough," I say.

"But that's not what I want to talk about," she says.

"Alright, what do you want to talk about?" I ask. I take another sip of my wine as I lean back into her couch, pulling my right leg up to let my ankle rest against my left knee.

"I was extremely distracted tonight while I was trying to be on a date with Clint," she says. "And it's your fault."

"How so?" I ask. "Did I say something concerning?"

"No," she says. "Nothing like that. I was distracted because I was thinking about you."

My entire body involuntarily perks up and I know she can sense it. If there was ever a time to try not to smile smugly, it would be now but I don't think I can help myself.

"Don't smile like that," she huffs, reading me like one of her books.

"I don't think I can stop," I say.

"The point is you ruined my date," she says.

"Or maybe I saved you," I counter, taking another sip from my glass.

Thea's mouth opens and then closes again. "Honestly, that's a strong possibility."

"What do you mean?" I ask.

"After we pulled into the restaurant, I told him I couldn't go through with the date and was sorry I wasted his time but didn't want to string him along further. He got mad and called me a charity case. He said I've got baggage and made me feel like he was doing me a favor."

"That's complete and utter bullshit," I say. My left-hand curls into a tight fist, and I'm so mad that I'm tempted to reach down deep into my past and find the violence I escaped.

"I know, I know," she says. "But it got to me for a moment. Then I realized I was relieved he revealed himself now rather than get too deep into it before I saw his true self."

"Silver linings," I say. "A good way to look at it."

"Yeah," she sighs. "Except now I'm mad at you."

I laugh again, shaking my head. "I don't see how that's my fault."

"Yes, yes, it is. I was content, perfectly content before you came along with all your pebbles and charm," she says. "Now, I'm in danger of making the same mistake I did in my youth."

"Which is?" I ask.

"Listen, you're a nice guy. You've been very sweet to me and kind to Ethan. But you're also very much like Shane."

"I'm nothing like Shane," I say, slightly annoyed by the comparison.

"I just mean you've got this bad boy vibe going, and you probably have a very related work schedule, and you live your life very freely. Plus, you're young. Like way younger than me. Which means you're still figuring your shit out, what you want in life and all that."

"I think you're getting ahead of yourself," I say. "I also think you're drawing a lot of conclusions about me based on what? The fact that I have tattoos?"

"No, no, of course not. I have tattoos myself. It's more just... I don't know. Your vibe," she says.

"I'm going to circle back to this vibe you're talking about but first I want to know about these tattoos you have," I say, grinning as I take another sip of my wine.

Thea rolls her eyes. "Of course you do."

"Hey, it's a strictly professional interest," I say, lying. But she knows that.

"Uh huh," she says. "Look, I was young when I got them. Shane talked me into them. And honestly, I need to cover up one of them."

"Which one?" I ask.

Thea slaps her palm against her forehead, clearly hating this topic.

"Just remember I was young, okay? And impressionable. And stupid," she says.

"I'm sure I've seen worse," I assure her.

Thea stands as she begins to pull the top of her leggings down, exposing her left thigh. Scrawled right across the top is Shane's name, inked in crude lettering. Honestly, it's awful and I'm both sad and angry that someone did that to her.

"Jesus," I say. "That's rough."

Thea nods, pulling her pants back up as she plops back down on the couch. Reaching for her glass on the coffee table, she tucks her hair behind her ear.

"I told you," she says.

"And I'm guessing getting it covered hasn't exactly been a priority," I say, understanding the sacrifice.

"Exactly," she says. "But I know what I'll get if I ever manage to do it."

Intrigued, I lean closer to her. "Do tell."

"It's probably really cliche to someone like you, but I'd love to fill my leg from the top of my thigh to my knee with wildflowers, really bright colors, very vibrant," she says.

"I don't think that's cliche," I shrug. "Flowers are symbolic of a lot of things for a lot of people. I never really judge what anyone wants. Except for that time a girl had Hawk tattoo a tiny smiling penis on her hip. We all judged that pretty hard."

"Oh my god," she says, starting to laugh. "That's awful."

"We know," I say, joining in the laughter.

A contented silence falls over us as the laughter dies. Thea takes another sip of her wine, tucking her hair back again. Something stirs inside me, but I can't put words to it. I want to ask her a million questions and watch the answers fall from her perfect mouth.

"Go on a date with me," I say. It's less a question and more a statement.

Thea's eyes find mine across the couch, her head tilting precariously to the side. It's as if she's looking for something, though I couldn't say what.

"One date," she says. "One date and if I don't want another, you never ask again."

A wry smile stretches over my face, and I definitely can't help it this time. "One date. And I'll stop."

"Deal," she says, sticking out her hand. "Shake on it."

At this moment, I decide to push for one more act of brazen idiocracy as I shift toward her, past her extended arm. My face couldn't be more than two inches from hers as I feel her breath against me.

"I'd rather kiss on it," I whisper. But then I wait. Because I'm not a fucking asshole who'd kiss her without knowing she wanted me to.

Her hesitation is clear, which causes me to second guess my boldness. Then, she nods ever so slightly. But it's just enough.

I lean in, gently pressing my lips to hers. I'm not on a mission for a full-blown make-out session. I just want a little taste. She presses back against me, my senses filled with heat and warmth and floral notes. And then it's over as we pull back from one another.

Thea bashfully presses her lips together, a flush of pink over her cheeks and the tip of her nose, as she suppresses a smile. I sink my teeth into my bottom lip, wishing it had lasted longer but knowing it definitely shouldn't.

"Oh my god, I can't believe I just kissed you," she says.

"Bad?" I ask, knowing full well she doesn't think so.

"Not at all," she says. "I just can't believe I did it."

"Regret?" I ask.

"Also no," she says. "But you should probably go."

Thea's legs flex beneath my hand resting on her knee as if she's checking to make sure they still function. They're tense like she's trying to hold them together.

"You're right," I say. "I should go."

We stand at the same time, stretching out the stiffness we likely both feel. It's late, we've got a little wine in us, and I don't know about her—although I could make an educated guess—I'm turned on brighter than a strobe light.

At the door, I hold out my arms, prompting her to lean into me for a hug. She grips my back as I wrap around her, catching that same light floral scent as before. It smells so soft, I'm tempted to ask her what it is and go buy it, but the more I consider it, the creepier I think it is.

I depart, promising to text her tomorrow about the date. One date. That's all I have to prove myself to her. One date seals our fate.

In many species of birds, the male puts on a very extravagant dancing display. But they only get one shot. If the female doesn't like what she sees, she moves on to the next one until she's satisfied.

So, I have to dance—metaphorically speaking. And I guaran-goddamn-tee you I'm going to do everything in my power not to blow it.

# KISS THE SKY

The smile plastered on my face hasn't subsided since the moment I left Thea James's doorstep. I smiled as I got into my car, and all the way home, and changing into shorts for bed, and fell peacefully to sleep smiling like a fool.

"So, what's this grand date going to be, Mr. Smiley?" Will teases as she rounds the counter to sit Ava's lunch down. "Ava, your lunch is ready!"

The faint sound of Ava's feet pad down the hallway as I rake my fingers through my hair. "I don't know, but it's gotta be good. And I need to figure it out soon because I promised I'd text her about it today."

Will slides a plate over to me and Derek before grabbing her own. Ava joins us at the counter moments later, and everyone is silent as if we're all thinking about what the date could be.

"Why don't you take her to that new restaurant downtown? It's supposed to be really good," Derek suggests.

I pick up the sandwich on my plate and take a bite, my head tilting side to side as I chew because I just don't think a classic dinner and movie or similar is going to cut it.

"I think it needs to be more interesting than that," Will chimes in, almost like she knows what I'm thinking.

"Me too," Ava says.

"Since when do you know what people should do on dates?" I ask.

Ava shrugs as she takes a second bite of her own sandwich. "I'm in middle school. I see things. I hear things."

"I don't even want to know what that means," Will says. "Kids these days are a different breed."

Hawk appears from the back room, looking pretty exhausted. He's spent a lot of time at his mom's house, helping her do everything from getting in and out of bed to cleaning the house and cooking for her. Drew takes care of tasks like helping her to the bathroom, getting dressed, and bathing. Right now, she can't get in and out of the shower or tub so it's been mostly sponge baths. From what I understand, Drew doesn't actually have to wash her but she's there to assist in the process.

"What are we talking about?" Hawk asks.

"I got a date with Thea," I say. "But I don't know what to do for the date."

"Congrats, man," he says, taking a plate from Will. "I'm sure whatever you decide, it will be great."

"That's just it," I say. "I need it to be better than great. I need epic."

"So skydiving?" Will suggests.

I know she's joking but the thought had crossed my mind. It can't be too over the top though like I'm trying too hard. It needs to be epic but meaningful.

"Maybe I'm overthinking this," I say. I pick up the pickle spear and take a bite, as it makes a satisfying crunching noise. In reality, I don't think she's expecting me to pull out all the stops and take her on an epic fantasy of a date. I'm sure she expects a nice, normal date. Which would be fine. But her expecting that is the exact reason I don't want to do it. It's just like the gifts I gave her—the pebbles. She gave me a regular list of "the same old stuff" and I thought outside the box to improve them. I feel like that's what I need to do in this instance as well.

"Why don't you just do what Hawk did?" Ava says, matter-of-factly.

"What did I do?" Hawk asks, looking down at her.

Ava sighs, clearly frustrated with our adult brains. I appreciate her unique perspective.

"On your first date with Mom, you gave her the tattoo you knew she wanted. You listened to her and gave her that gift. That's all anyone wants, right? To feel heard?" Ava looks at each of our faces, all of which I'm sure are displaying varying degrees of shock.

"It's true," Will says. "It's all any woman wants."

I absorb the wisdom of an eleven-year-old, clearly wise beyond her years, and try to recall the details of all the conversations I've had with Thea. Aside from last night, most of them haven't traveled beyond the surface. Although, I do know she needs a tattoo. She definitely said that. Perhaps I could pull directly from Hawk's playbook.

"Hawk," I say. "I'll probably be in the shop one evening this week."

"No problem, man," he says, clapping me on the shoulder. He leans in close, whispering out of Ava's earshot. "Just don't have sex on the front counter. I've already had to replace it once after Drew and I stayed late."

"I didn't need to know that, thank you," I say, laughing. "Solid advice."

Excusing myself from the counter, I walk through the living room and out onto the balcony as I whip out my phone. I don't want to wait any longer to text Thea. It's been long enough. I actually had to stop myself from texting her last night and first thing this morning, which is weird for me.

ME: I've got a plan, *deusa*.

THEA: I was wondering when I was going to hear from you.

ME: I'm sorry I kept you waiting.

THEA: It's ok, although I was starting to think you were backing out.

ME: I would literally never.

THEA: So what's the plan?

ME: When are you free?

THEA: Wednesday evening?

ME: Perfect, I'll pick you up at six if that works?

THEA: I can make that work. Where are we going?

ME: I can't tell you that.

THEA: Can you at least tell me what I should wear?

My fingers hover over the keyboard as I consider her question. I understand she wants to dress appropriately for the evening but I'm not in favor of feeling like I'm dictating what a woman wears.

ME: I want you to reach all the way back into your closet and choose one of those outfits you never wear but desperately want a reason to.

THEA: How did you know I have those outfits?

ME: Because every woman does.

THEA: You're dangerous.

ME: Yes, but I'm the right kind of dangerous.

I put my phone away as I look out across the street, observing all the people going about their lives. I can't put a finger on it, but there's something peaceful at this moment.

Male Bowerbirds spend months meticulously preparing towers made of twigs and other materials. They adorn them with flower petals, stones, and even glass or berries. If a female shows interest, he'll begin vocalizing for her, singing lullabies to seal the deal. It's truly a maximum effort situation. He understands he must work hard because the female will settle for nothing less.

Thea James deserves the maximum effort. It's as simple as that.

## INTERLUDE

### THEA

Webster's doesn't have a term for what I'm feeling today. It doesn't have one for what I felt the other night when I blindly invited Hanson over either. Someone needs to come up with a word for "I'm so nervous I'm shitting my proverbial pants" and that will be close enough.

What's worse is I can't wipe the stupid smile from my lips —the same lips he kissed so tenderly I could've cried. Several students have asked me what's wrong with my face. And for that matter, some staff have as well. Both of which have caused me a considerable amount of concern as to what my face normally looks like.

Last night, I sat down with Ethan to ask him his honest thoughts about Hanson and me dating in general. Kids are so much more resilient than we give them credit for. I explained I have a date tonight, that he'd be with his dad like normal, and that if he wasn't comfortable with it, I wouldn't go. His response was—and I'm paraphrasing, of course—that I should do what makes me happy and pointed out that his dad dates so I can too.

I re-confirmed with Hanson after that conversation and again about twenty minutes ago. As for a total, I'd say I've double and triple-checked with him around five times. His standard response is now a smiling emoji and the words, "Yes, I'm still sure."

This morning I reached into the back of my closet, as prescribed. How he knew it was there and who taught him of our closet habits, I may never know. Still, I pulled the violet mini dress from the depths of my collection and hung it on the back of my bathroom door for later. I just pray it's okay for what he has planned.

"Miss James?" Ava's sweet voice interrupts my thoughts, her big eyes looking up at me quizzically.

"Yes, Ava, what can I do for you?" I ask.

"I was just making sure you're okay," she says. "I'm finished with my test."

She hands me the stapled packet with pride before returning to her seat. We both already know she did well. I'll tell you, if the school did have a math team, she'd be the team captain.

Checking the clock, I realize I've been staring blankly into space and thinking about Hanson's kiss and that blasted dress for the better part of thirty minutes. Time certainly flies when you're shitting your pants.

I'm starting to regret not having more girlfriends to talk to. When we moved here, I was still neck-deep in Shane's bullshit and didn't feel like confiding about it to anyone. After we divorced, it had been so long that it felt strange to walk up to my coworkers and say, "Sorry about the last several years, I was in a terrible marriage, can we be friends now?" As a result, I'm a little light on genuine connection.

Ten minutes until I need to call time on the test and my mind is reeling. Maybe tonight is a terrible idea or maybe it's a great one. All I know is there's a strange part of me that hopes he's shitting his pants too.

---

The violet mini dress is on, paired with black pumps, and I've already stuffed my essentials into a black clutch to match. As I examine myself in the mirror for the hundredth time, I can't help but make a list in my head of all the flaws I see. This dress hugs me, pushing my ladies up for display and clinging to everything south until the fabric abruptly ends mid-thigh. I didn't say this was a family-friendly dress.

A knock on my door nearly causes me to jab myself with my eyeliner and I briefly play out a scenario in which I wear a pirate's patch for the evening. My heart begins to do what I can only describe as belly flops into the pit of my stomach as I scramble to throw on my jewelry last minute.

Grabbing my purse, I head toward the front door, trying my best to calm myself down before opening it. Through the small window on my door, I can't see anything but the back of Hanson's head, which does nothing to ease my worries.

Twisting the knob, I inhale deeply and forget to release

until my eyes meet his. Holy hell. Hanson. Is. Wearing. A. Suit. Like a whole ass suit. My nerves about my attire dissipate a little, realizing my dress is on par with what he's wearing.

There's something about seeing a man wearing ripped jeans and tight-fitted shirts on so many occasions and then bam! He hits you with this—a black jacket and matching vest over a white shirt and black tie. His black pants that seem to hug his thighs and ass so perfectly there's no way it's off the rack. I stop myself from spiraling too far and wondering why such a young guy would have a suit this nice.

"Hello, beautiful," he says, extending his hand toward mine.

"Hello to you as well," I say, allowing him to take my hand into his.

He pulls the back of my knuckles to his lips, placing three firm kisses against them. Heat travels down the center of me and, on the outside, a blush has likely formed over my cheeks and chest.

Inside, however, I'm panting like a dog in heat. And yes, I realize how unbelievably vulgar that sounds but this man.

This goddamn man.

## LOST IN THE MOMENT
### THEA

I'm not even a little ashamed to admit that upon seeing him at the door, I excused myself for a moment pretending to have forgotten something. As he waited for me in the living room, I ran into my bathroom and hiked up my dress, tucking it beneath my chin. Grabbing a magazine from the counter, I spread my legs as wide as I could without toppling over and used it to fan my inner thighs and lady bits. I'm also not ashamed to admit that I briefly considered trying to rub one out at record speed but ultimately ruled against it.

"Ready to go?" he asks, buckling his seatbelt.

I nod, mostly just relieved to have finally made it out to the car. "Yes, I'm ready."

"How was your day?" he asks.

Earlier, he let me know he wouldn't be the one picking Ava up because he was caught up at work on something. The news came with more disappointment than expected which very much surprised me. So, this is the first time I'm seeing him today. "It was pretty good, although I almost had to cancel the date altogether."

"Why's that?" he asks.

"Shane gave me a hard time earlier. He said he couldn't come to get Ethan until much later and I argued with him about how unacceptable that was. The only compromise available was me driving him over." I huff as I recall the ordeal.

"That's rough," he says. "I'm sorry."

"It's life," I say. "Unfortunately, it's not the first or last time it will happen. So, I've officially given you fair warning."

"Noted," he laughs. "But you're here now so you have a choice to make."

"And what's that?" I ask, genuinely curious.

"We can do the activity portion of the night first, or dinner first," he says. "It's your call."

"And I assume I don't get to know what either involves?" I ask.

"I'll give you one bit of information," he says. "If we eat first, you can't drink alcohol before the event. So, you'd have to get something else first. Then, you can drink after. Or we do the activity first, then drink and eat after."

"Well, that's certainly intriguing," I muse. "An activity I have to be sober for, what could it be?"

"I can't tell," he says. "But I need your decision in the next forty-five seconds to make the appropriate turn."

Oh god, now I'm on a clock. "This is a very stressful start." I laugh. Doesn't he know how indecisive women can be when forced to make decisions about what they want? I consider all information—despite how limited it is. On the one hand, I'm starving and haven't eaten since ten this morning. I'm blaming that on the nerves as well. And while I've never been a huge drinker, I was hoping for a cocktail with dinner to help settle the aforementioned nerves. Then again, the idea of an activity where drinking simply cannot happen is driving me mad.

"Let's eat first," I say, ultimately knowing my empty belly will only add to my nerves and the idea of fainting on this date doesn't appeal to me.

"As you wish," he says, taking the next right turn which puts us in the direction of downtown.

"May I ask where we're going to eat?" I say.

"No," he says. "But I hope you're an adventurous eater."

Great. I've had to make decisions, and I don't even know if I'm going to like the food he's chosen doesn't seem like an awesome start to the date.

Just as my thoughts threaten to turn sour about this experience, Hanson's hand finds mine resting on my knee. As his fingers hook around, caressing my palm, all energy causing my body to be tense and rigid melts away.

My eyes wander from our joined hands up his arm until they meet his. He gives me a genuine, confident smile and suddenly I couldn't care less about what we're going to eat. It could be hot dogs from a cart vendor near the football stadium and I'd happily squirt ketchup on that thing and call it delicious.

Which is what frightens me. Shane had that kind of power over me once upon a time because I pulled back the curtain on who he truly was, or still is, I should say.

The point is, I have a type. I have a very specific type who I will let walk all over me and then I'll thank them for it. And that's exactly why I was in search of a nice, reliable guy who was nothing like Shane. Although that backfired in a way I never predicted, so who the hell knows. Maybe it's me. Maybe I simply attract the worst kinds of people.

"Tell me something about you," Hanson says, thankfully interrupting that spiral.

"Like what?" I ask.

"Anything you want," he says. "Something you haven't told me before. We've got a few minutes before we arrive at the restaurant."

Ah, he said restaurant and not hot dog cart, so I guess I'm in luck. I ponder his question for a moment, wondering how deep to take this or if I should start with something on the surface. "I hate feet."

Hanson laughs. "You mean touching them?"

"Touching them, looking at them, smelling them, you name it," I say. "I taught Ethan how to do his laundry just so I didn't have to touch his socks. His baby socks were fine but his preteen socks are the stuff of nightmares."

"So, you're saying I can't put my feet in your lap when we're relaxing on the couch?" he asks, laughing again.

"I will throw up on you," I say, starting to laugh at myself.

"I'm making an extra special note of that," he says. "No feet. Got it."

"Now your turn," I say.

Hanson's quiet for several long minutes as a look of contemplation washes over his face. If I didn't know better, I'd say he's wading through some more serious confessions than mine.

"I have been seeing a therapist for a few years," he says.

It only takes me a split second to adjust to this information, which I consider very intimate. Mental health is important, and not something to be poked fun at. Men, in particular, often don't seek therapy when they should, because society has regarded it as a sign of weakness to them. "That's great," I say. "I assume if it's been that long, it's helpful to you?"

"Yes, I think so," he says. "Although, I still have a ways to go."

I'm tempted to ask why he goes, and what he needs a therapist for, but I don't push it. The mere act of telling me he sees a therapist is enough for now.

"I saw a therapist for about two years after Ethan was born," I say. "I was suffering from some postpartum depression and emotions that I needed help with."

"Really?" he asks.

"Yes, but I feel much better now, though I do have her saved in my contacts and have checked in with her from time to time," I say. "I always begged Shane to consider seeing someone but he refused."

"Not surprising," he says.

"I'm sorry," I say. "That's the last time I'll be mentioning Shane. Two times on one date is enough." I laugh, trying to lighten the tone. I don't like to talk about Shane or our problems on dates, especially the early ones. But sometimes the conversation veers that way without warning.

"I don't mind," he says. "He was and still is a big part of

your life in many ways. I think anyone who takes you on a date should realize that."

You would think. You would fucking think. But I've been told on more than one occasion by a date that they were tired of hearing about him. What they don't realize is the moment you ask me a question about myself, my past, or my child, you're probably going to hear his name at least once. Do I hate it? Yes. But it is what it is.

"We're here," he says, pulling into the parking lot of a restaurant I've never heard of. "It's a Brazilian steakhouse, an authentic one. I thought I'd give you a little taste of me," Hanson says, winking.

He knows what he did there. He knows full well that was a sexually charged innuendo. On any other date, with any other man, I'd have expressed my disdain. On this one? I have no disdain. I'm searching around for it and coming up empty. Disdain has left the building. I give him my best teasing smile.

Watch out, world. Thea James is a flirt.

## DIRTY PAWS
### HANSON

I could think of no better place for us to eat than the Brazilian steakhouse downtown. The food is exquisite and authentic, which is hard to come by. It also boasts a very intimate environment mixed with unexplainable electricity in the air.

Of course, the dancers may be part of it. On the weekends, the place hosts many professional dancers, couples with chemistry so intense that their choreographed movements feel very real. They float around on the floor as if they don't even have legs. Thea's face lit up each time a new couple made their way around, moving and touching to seductive music. The dancers themselves are also Brazilian, each putting their twist on the Samba and other native dances.

"That food was amazing," she says. "If that's what you ate every day you lived there, I don't know why you ever left."

I laugh, attempting to mask my unease at the comment.

It's not as if she did it on purpose, she doesn't know. But the reasons I left far outweigh the food, of that I can assure you.

"And are we ready for our activity?" I ask.

"Yes, definitely," she says. "Unless you're going to try to make me dance like those women back there."

I laugh. "Not quite. Maybe that'll be our next date."

"Please no," she laughs. "They're in far better shape than I am. I'll look like a cartwheeling potato trying to do that."

Except I don't laugh at that comment. "You don't think you look like a potato, do you?"

"Compared to those women? Yes. Compared to actual potatoes? Almost," she says, laughing again at her own expense.

"Thea," I say, my tone more serious as I breathe her name.

"Yes?" she says.

"I want you to know something," I say, pulling into the parking lot of Bird's Eye at exactly the right moment. I turn the car off, unbuckling my seatbelt so I can turn toward her more directly. "And I want you to hear me. Hear me."

"What is it?" she asks, the muscles in her throat working as she swallows.

"You are the most exquisite woman I've ever met," I pause. "And that goes for every part of you, inside and out."

Thea's eyes dart away from mine, and in the dim lighting of a distant streetlamp, her eyes brim with tears.

"That's the nicest thing anyone's ever said to me," she says. "I've got a lot of self-image issues."

Her confession hits me like a ton of bricks. I don't know

who made her feel this way about herself, and my guess is Shane was a major player, but I hate it. All of it.

"May I be uncharacteristically blunt with you?" I ask, knowing sometimes that's what it takes to get through these situations.

"Yes," she whispers, still attempting to hold back her emotions.

"You have the most perfect ass I've ever seen," I say. "And maybe it won't be tonight, but if you ever gift me the privilege of touching it, I may never wash my hands again."

My words are true but silly, and with them comes a burst of laughter from her throat. It's the reaction I was hoping for. It's true and carries the potential for a hot moment, but within my presentation also lies the ability to break this tension.

At the end of the day, I know it doesn't matter what I say. Women will always see themselves one way, while most see them in a very different way. All we can hope to do is close the gap between their reality and ours, even if it's just a little.

―――

"What are we doing here?" she asks as I unlock the door to the shop and let her stop in.

I lock the door behind us as I flip on one of the overhead lights. "This is where our activity will take place."

Grabbing her hand, I pull her over to my workstation, pointing out my certificate and the art hanging inside my booth.

"You're very talented," she says.

"I'm glad you think so," I say. "Take a look at this one."

I point to a sketch sitting on my tattoo chair, the one I worked on all day and I watch as she picks it up, running her fingers over the lines. The bouquet of wildflowers in itself wasn't difficult. I tried to create the shape of it from memory, making sure it would cover her thigh in such a way that it would hide all of her old tattoos.

"What's this for?" she asks.

"I know I've already given you flours once," I say. "And perhaps most would've shown up to your doorstep with real flowers for a first actual date. But tonight, if you'll let me, I'd like to give you this bouquet instead. Tonight, I'd like to give you the gift of loving a part of your body again."

As I say this, I step closer to her, trailing my fingers over the top part of her thigh where I know a name haunts her. And for a second time tonight, I've moved Thea James to near tears.

―――

Pulling my gloves off at the end of the session, I look down at the now bandaged section of her leg. To my surprise, she's a champion in the chair. She didn't complain a single time and didn't even request a break.

"All done," I say. "Here's some stuff to care for it at home." I hand her a small bag with ointment and care instructions, in case I'm not around to answer her questions at some point.

"Thank you," she says. "Thank you so much. I'd put that

off for so long and now that it's done, I'm floored. It's more beautiful than I ever expected."

"You're welcome," I say. "I'm glad you like it."

"Like doesn't even cover it," she says. "I love it."

I smile at her as I clean up my station, knowing this was more than a tattoo for her. And that's what I love about my job. Sometimes someone comes along and it's more than a little ink to them—it's therapy. It's remembering or forgetting. It's a second chance.

Thea walks to the mirror, and even though it's already bandaged, she still examines her leg in the mirror. Her dress is pulled up to her hips and though I did my best to keep it as professional as possible, it was hard to ignore the lace edge of her black panties in such proximity to where I was tattooing.

"So, can we have a nightcap?" she asks.

"Sure, there's a place down the street-"

"No," she says, interrupting me. "At my place?"

Oh. Oohhhhhh. Okay, yes. "Sure," I say, reaching to turn out the light above my booth. "Let me just grab something from the back."

Now, I'm not proud of what I'm about to do. But I happen to know that in the very back of the stock room, there's a jar of condoms. I didn't personally carry condoms on me or in my car for this date because I didn't think there was a snowball's chance in hell it was happening. But while a nightcap back at her place isn't a guarantee of sex, it does mean it's possible, planned or not. And the thought of arriving at that moment unprepared would be the saddest moment in my personal recent history.

After grabbing a handful and shoving them into my pocket, I lock up the shop and we head back to her place. It's quiet in the car, but not awkward. I imagine we're both wondering if this is a good idea. Or if she's like me, she's wondering if we can have sex without putting her leg through too much pain. Fuck, she's probably not thinking that, you idiot.

Before I know it, we're back in her living room the way we were the night I came over with wine. Only this time, she's not wearing oversized sweatpants and a loose-fitting T-shirt. Instead, she's in shorts so short the bottom edge of her bandage can be seen and a tank top that hides nothing. It's not hot in her house, but it is hot in here—inside my body. Despite removing my suit jacket, rolling up my sleeves, and removing my shoes... I. Am. Hot. And it has nothing to do with the thermostat.

"Here you go," she says, handing me a glass of amber liquid.

It's certainly not the light, sippable wine we had before. "Thank you." Perhaps we both know tonight warrants something with a bit more bite.

"So," she says. "Is this the part where I tell you another thing you don't know about me?"

"If you want it to be," I say, sipping from my glass. Given this is Kentucky, I should've guessed it's bourbon. But I'm unclear what kind, though the taste is smooth and smoky.

She sips from her glass, a gentle smile curling up the edges of her mouth. At the beginning of the night, each strand of her hair was curled perfectly into place. Now, it's swept back into a ponytail with loose baby strands at the back of her neck and framing the sides of her face. She's swiped most of the makeup away, as well, and I appreciate the comfort she shows in doing that.

"I've only had sex with three men," she says. "Shane was my first. There was one shortly after. And then a guy I dated for a short time a little over two years ago. That's it."

I'm shocked. Not at the number but more so at her willingness to talk about it. "Is that supposed to be bad?"

"No," she says. "I don't think so. Well, I guess maybe, depending on how you look at it."

"How do you look at it?" I ask.

"Like I'm in my mid-thirties and have less sexual experience than some teens half my age," she says, sighing.

"So, you're saying you wish you had more?" I ask, making sure to clarify, given the sensitivity of the subject.

"I'm saying yes, I wish I'd slutted it up in my youth," she says, laughing.

"There's still time," I say.

"Perhaps," she says, taking another sip.

I contemplate how much trust she has in me to tell me something like that, and realize even though this is technically only our first date, our unique path here helped aid in that.

My mouth starts to water at the thought of what my brain is willing me to say. My hand grips the glass a little tighter as I pop my neck in preparation for unloading this.

"My father is in prison," I say. I let the words linger for a moment, suspended in the air between us. "And I put him there."

## KISS ME SLOWLY
### THEA

The term speechless doesn't even begin to cover what I'm feeling at this moment. Hanson's father is in prison. Hanson put him there. I have what feels like an infinite number of questions I want answers to—all of which range from how in the hell to why in the world, but there's only one I truly need the answer to.

"Are you okay?" I ask, leaning forward. My hand brushes over his forearm, coming to rest near his wrist.

"Most of the time," he says.

I appreciate the honesty in his answer. "That's all we can really hope for."

"You don't have any questions?" he asks.

"Of course I do," I say. "I think anyone would. But I imagine you know what they are and if you're not ready to answer them, that's more than fine. I'm sure when you tell people this, they just start spewing them."

He's quiet for a moment as he shifts on his side of the

couch, taking another sip of his drink and then placing his glass on the coffee table. It's as if we're going in slow motion now, but time behaves differently when shit gets really real really fast.

"You're the third person in my life I've told," he says. "My therapist, Avery, and you. That's it."

"Wow," I say.

Hanson edges closer to me on the couch, his legs beginning to press against mine. The heat I felt earlier today resurfaces with a vengeance, spreading like wildfire from my throat all the way down to my lady bits.

"Thea," he breathes.

The way he says my name—somewhere between an exhale and a whisper—is more than I can bear. His eyes travel to my mouth and it doesn't feel like he's moving but he's inexplicably closer than a moment ago.

"Hanson," I say, my voice cracking.

"I think I'd like to kiss you again," he says.

It's not a question but he's still waiting for permission. His advance is halted, teetering and dependent on my next words.

I close my eyes, the warmth of his breath tickling my skin. He runs the fingertips of his right hand in circles on my knee, waiting.

"Yes." It's the only word he needs, his mouth connecting to mine a fraction of a moment later. I lean back further against the armrest as his hands find my waist. I part my lips for him, his tongue lapping at mine.

Somehow and suddenly, we're horizontal. I can't recount the logistics of the transition, but I know it was smooth.

Hanson's got one hand above him, holding himself in place by gripping the edge of the couch. His other caresses my back and sides with each slow kiss—threatening to pull something from me I've long thought was nonexistent.

My thighs press together as I try to contain everything I'm feeling. It's clawing its way to the surface—an animal I can't keep caged much longer.

Hanson pulls back, breaking the kiss between us.

"What's wrong, love?" he asks.

"Nothing," I say, reaching up toward him.

"I can feel it, you know," he whispers, leaning down to place his lips near my ear. "I can feel your body, *deusa*. I can feel it begging."

I don't even have words. As his hips grind against mine, all that escapes me are whimpering sounds.

"I can make you feel good," he whispers. "If you'll let me."

My hands clench into fists on either side of my body as I try to contain everything. Because I want to let Hanson Serrano make me feel good. I haven't felt good in so long. But what kind of Pandora's Box will be unleashed if I let him in?

He presses a single kiss to my mouth, nibbling my bottom lip before pulling back again to make eye contact as he grinds against me again. My back arches toward him and I have to choose. Stop this cold where it is or unleash everything. There is no in-between.

"Make me feel good," I whisper. "I want you to make me feel everything."

A wry smile plays over his lips as if I've just issued a challenge. And maybe I have.

"Give me a word," he says.

"What word?" I ask, my breath already ragged.

"Any word," he says. "A safe word."

"Oh my god, what?" I shudder again as his knee parts my legs.

"Don't worry, love. Just a word I'll listen for. You say it and no matter what, I'll stop," I say.

"Uhm, uh," I fumble. *A word, Thea. Think of a fucking word.* Jesus Christ, I've never needed a safe word for sex. How kinky is this about to get? Whips? Chains? Gags? "Malarky!" I exclaim with much too enthusiasm.

Hanson stops all movement, laughing a little. "Did you just say malarky?"

"What?" I say. "It's a word."

"Yes, love. It's a word," he says. "Malarky it is."

Hanson begins the grinding motion from before but I'm not finished defending my word. "Personally, I don't think malarky gets enough love. It's a good word."

"Thea," he whispers, doing that thing with my name that makes my insides flip.

"Yes?" I say.

"Are you nervous?" he asks.

"No, of course not," I say, then immediately correct myself. "Well, maybe a little but that's only because I've never needed a safe word for sex and like I said before, I'm not what most would consider super experienced so-"

"Relax," he says, quieting me. "Would you like to go to your bedroom?"

I nod, thinking better of trying to have the type of sex that requires a safe word on this couch.

He stands, extending his hand to help me up, and waits to follow behind me as I walk down the hallway toward my room.

Just a few steps from the couch, he stops me, wrapping his arm around my waist and kissing my neck.

"Take off your tank top," he says, loosening his grip for me to remove it. Once gone, his fingertips trail my spine as I walk a few more steps. He digs his hands into my hips, nibbling my bare shoulder.

"Now your shorts," he commands.

I push them down over my hips and step out when they fall to the floor. I make it to my bedroom door, but his hand halts mine on the knob.

"And your panties," he says, his lips against my earlobe.

"You're still wearing all your clothes," I protest.

"Don't worry," he says. "You're going to take those off too."

Swallowing down the lump in my throat, I finger the elastic edge of my panties, before pushing them down. They catch on my thighs but he stops me from reaching down.

"I'll get that," he says.

As he kneels, he spins me around to face him. His hands make quick work of getting my panties down and helping me step out of them. Though, he doesn't discard them to the floor but rather tucks them into the pocket on his vest.

"What are you doing?" I ask, giggling. It's not a weird

laugh, more so an intimate one. I think laughing during sexy time is a wonderful thing.

"We will need them later," he says, but his eyes don't meet mine.

He's too busy staring directly at my lady bits. In fact, he's licking his lips. One of his hands has a grip on the backside of my knee, while the other has gone rogue, making its way up my now parted legs.

"Close your eyes," he says.

I do as instructed, the thumb of his hand occasionally pressing into my flesh. It trails farther and farther up, coming to rest just beyond the center of me.

"Spread your legs wider," he says.

My knees wobble as I widen my stance.

"Good girl," he whispers.

Ugh. That's almost too much for me to handle. The backs of his knuckles graze my most sensitive skin, my body shuddering at the brief contact.

Then, all at once, two fingers glide over me with fervent intention. There's no stopping the moan as it escapes my mouth. I don't even try. His fingers glide over me again, this time more slowly. Then again. They stop mid-stroke and go in the opposite direction. The next thing I know, they're swiping over me again and again, my knees all but bucking under the pleasure.

I grip his shoulder, certain I'm about to orgasm just like this. No part of him is inside me but I'm so close I can feel it beginning to build.

Then, his touch is gone. Hanson is back on his feet, kissing my lips as I finally open my eyes.

"What are you doing?" I ask. "I was almost there."

"I know, love," he says, smiling. "I told you I can feel it."

"Then why did you stop?" I ask. For whatever reason, my intended tone isn't present. Instead, I'm whining, begging.

"We're not even in the bedroom yet," he says. "We're in no rush. We have plenty of time."

Hanson may have plenty of time, but I certainly do not. At least that's what my body is telling me. It's literally screaming at me as I walk into my room stark naked. NOW! NOW! GIVE US THE ORGASM RIGHT NOW!

"Sit right here," he says, motioning to the edge of the bed. "And you can undress me now."

Yes, okay. I can do this. I can undress him. That means I'm in charge. Even as I think it, I don't believe it. I unbutton his vest, pushing it from his shoulders. He removes the panties from earlier, laying them aside. Then, I unbutton his shirt, his tattooed torso slowly emerging from behind the crisp white shirt.

That…is a very sexy torso. Hanson doesn't have the type of muscles you see in magazines. He's not super lean like a swimmer. His frame is thicker, solid, and hard. My fingers explore the edges of his hips and along the sides of his ribcage. Everything is rigid, tense under my touch.

If there was ever going to be a body that could handle mine, it's this one.

## SHE IS LOVE

### HANSON

There's a trembling in my chest, a faint but fast-growing rumble. I don't know what it is or what it means, but I know it gets a little bit louder the moment my eyes connect with Thea's as she looks up at me in all her naked glory.

I take the condoms from my pocket, discarding them next to her panties on the edge of the bed. The sound of the zipper on my pants being undone by her trembling hands is the only thing I can hear aside from my erratically beating heart.

There isn't much time to think about all of it as my pants and boxer briefs hit the floor moments later. My hardened cock is free from constraint and I can't help but look at Thea's reaction to me. Her teeth dig into her bottom lip as if she's holding back and my ego is thoroughly stroked. Now let's see if I can get her to act on whatever thoughts are swimming around that pretty little head of hers.

"Thea," I whisper.

"Yes?" she says, looking up at me with those big hazel eyes I could melt for.

"Scoot back and lie down," I say.

She pulls her feet onto the bed, inching back until her head meets the pillow. Her legs aren't pressed together, not spread apart either. I watch as her hands fidget, attempting to find a resting spot.

"Are you okay?" I ask, pressing my knee onto the bed. Slowly crawling toward her, I don't take my eyes from hers.

"Yes," she says. It's barely audible, her voice cracking under her nerves. I want to ask if she's sure but I stop myself. She has her word. Though I'd prefer not to hear it tonight.

I run my hands over the tops of her thighs, gently encouraging her to part her legs. She does so, though not far enough.

"Wider," I say, still not breaking eye contact.

As she fulfills my request, my hands press into the flesh on either side of her center. Hearing the sharp exhale from her lungs only intensifies my hunger for her. Delicately, I trace a single fingertip over her clit, watching her shudder. It's the smallest moment of connection, but it packs a punch.

She twists, first away from the touch, then toward it. Her body can't decide whether to flee or feel and the place between the two is central to pleasure. My finger runs over her again and again. I don't change course and I don't pick up the pace. It's the same slow, deliberate movement each time.

Thea's eyelashes flutter open and closed, open again. Her breathing quickens as small noises escape her mouth. They're not quite moans, not yet. But we'll get there.

The same finger dips lower, feeling her wetness but still

not pushing inside of her. And wet she is, physical confirmation of her desire. After a couple more strokes, I pull back just far enough to hold three fingers together and deliver a firm smack to the same spot I've been rubbing.

Thea yelps, her head darting up from the pillow. She looks at me, eyes wild, then to where my hand is still cupping her. She's rattled, slightly shocked—which is exactly the effect I wanted it to have.

"Something wrong?" I ask, smiling like the devil on his birthday.

"No," she says. "I don't think so."

As she speaks her last word, I smack her again the same way as before, causing her to yelp again.

"Do you like that?" I ask.

She nods, attempting to press her lips together as ragged breaths escape her.

"I want to hear you say it," I say.

Thea's eyes close, her head falling back against the pillow again. But she doesn't get off that easy. I smack her again, this time a fraction harder, causing her eyes to shoot back open. She arches toward me this time, pressing herself into the palm of my hand.

"I like it," she says, breathlessly.

I feel a key turning deep inside me, a box I locked a long time ago. There's a delicious satisfaction in delivering pleasure to someone else—a visceral, almost animalistic hunger for me. I need it. I crave it above most other things. But I locked it away, reserving it for only very special occasions. And until

Thea James walked into my life, I'd seldom let it see the light of day.

"Good," I whisper. "That's good." My fingertips run over her one last time before I shift my body so that I can taste her. I'd be lying if I said I hadn't thought about this exact moment.

My mouth mere inches from her pussy, I look into her eyes one last time as I blow warm air against her. Her muscles tense all over her body, back arching. If she could burst from her skin, I have no doubt she would. Thea is writhing and I'm sure she's never been pushed this far before.

Her hand finds mine on her lower stomach, fingers lacing —a comfort measure. If I thought I appreciated the way she looked before when she was in her pajamas, make-up removed, then I don't know what to call this feeling now. Thea's twisted in knots, silently begging for release.

All at once, I plunge my tongue into her, covering her with the full of my mouth. I push further in, drag slowly out, then back in again. Her knees stiffen, then buckle as her hips begin to twist as if she's pulling away but my grip on her hips tightens, pulling her back to me.

I spread her legs wider, flattening my tongue against her opening as I alternate licking and sucking. She digs her heels into the mattress, pushing against me and then attempting to pull back but I won't let her go. Finally, she surrenders, her body beginning to rock into me in a steady rhythm. She likes this. She wants more of this. But I can't let her have it all, not yet.

Thea's hands grip the sheet on either side of her as she begins to rock harder and faster against my mouth. I suck her clit into my mouth, savoring her taste. If I do this maybe thirty seconds longer, she's going to orgasm before I ever even make it inside her. So, I pull away because that simply won't do.

A groan escapes her, and I'm beginning to think she doesn't like edging but then I watch a devious smile spread over her pretty mouth, curling up at the edges. It's absolutely wicked.

"Stop doing that," she says, breathing hard now.

I reach for a condom, intending to do exactly that but before I can slide it over me, she's reaching her hand around my cock as she leans up from the pillow. In one smooth motion, she wraps her lips around me, sucking as she swirls her tongue around the tip. Now I'm the one breathless, panting as I make every attempt to keep myself upright.

If I wasn't primed before, there's no doubt I am now. Despite her confessional claims about being inexperienced, she clearly possesses a naturally talented mouth. Shutting my eyes for a moment, my head falls back as I let myself go to the pleasure building inside. My hips rock against her as her mouth glides over me again and again.

Then, I push her away, pressing her back down onto the bed. Finally, I can see the hunger manifesting on her face, her hooded eyes dark and wanting.

"Put your hands above your head," I say. "Hold onto those rails and don't let go."

Thea wraps her hands around the wooden poles of her headboard, never once taking her eyes from mine. She's learning. She's ready.

"Remember the word?" I ask.

"I remember," she says.

Finishing what I started earlier, I discard the condom wrapper to the side of the bed and roll it over me. Her eyes move from my face to my hand on my dick so I tease her, stroking myself a few times for her benefit. Despite the temptation, her hands don't leave the frame.

With her panties within reach, I position myself between her legs, dragging my hard cock over her clit. She pushes toward me, nearly bucking.

Finally, I give her what I know she wants. Sliding in gently, I watch her eyes roll back as she holds her breath. I drag back out, then push into her again. Each time, the noise grows. A breath turns to a whimper, a whimper to a moan. I quicken my pace, pushing harder and faster until I hear the first scream.

Grabbing the black lace panties I took from her earlier, I ball them up inside my hand.

"Open your mouth," I say.

Without hesitation, her lips part and I stuff the panties in, careful not to gag her. That's not the objective. But she can't close her mouth now, her muffled noises dissipating into the air.

I lift both of her legs up, her ankles coming to rest on my shoulders. "Would you like to know what *deusa* means now?" As the words leave my mouth, I push myself inside her again slowly, letting her feel every inch.

She nods, the only response permitted by her makeshift gag. There's something wholly sexy about the fact that she could push them from her mouth at any time or let go of her bed frame but chooses to do neither.

I pause, allowing her legs to fall to either side of me as I lean down to kiss her cheek. I kiss her again and let my teeth graze her skin. It's a gentle moment, placed deliberately in juxtaposition to what has happened and what will happen when it's over.

Biting and kissing my way up her jawline until I reach her ear, I press my lips close. "It means goddess," I whisper, a growl forming low in my throat. "Because I've thought about this moment since the beginning. That I might get to worship you...with every...part...of...my body." My words fall in rhythm with each thrust, the noises coming from her fueling me.

She doesn't know it yet, but I'm only getting started.

## DAMN REGRET

### THEA

Euphoria. That's what this is. Bliss. Elation. Call it whatever you want. I'm calling it The Hanson Special.

His eyes roam my body, from my breasts bouncing to my eyes and back down to where our bodies connect. I watch his expression as he watches himself slide in and out of me. It's hot. Like the hottest thing I've ever experienced.

My hands still grasping the bed, I begin to push back harder against him, our bodies colliding in rhythm at the exact right moments. I've heard about sex like this, and even read it in a few romance novels. But I've never experienced anything like it until now.

Hanson's movements are so smooth and deliberate like he knows my body better than I do. Maybe he does. I swear I don't know anything anymore, especially not in this fuzzy drunken-like state of mind.

The delicious sensation that began to build earlier is

starting again, like a little volcano deep in my belly. And, as if on cue, Hanson's lips begin to curl into a devilish grin. See. He knows.

"Don't worry, *deusa*," he whispers. "I won't stop this time."

His words actually bring me a lot of relief, as I don't think I could survive being deprived again.

I close my eyes as I feel his hand slide from my hip to my tit. He rubs his thumb in a circle around my nipple, barely grazing the sensitive flesh. Then, without warning, he pinches it between his fingertips.

"Oh my god," I say, barely able to get the words out. Everything he does is pure magic.

He pinches again, squeezing and twisting, as my body writhes beneath his touch. Then, his index finger trails down my sternum and past my belly button.

I open my eyes to find him still watching my face. Our eyes connect and neither of us looks away. There's hunger in his gaze, something carnal. But beyond that, there's intimacy as well.

"Are you going to come for me, *deusa*?" he asks.

Yes. Absolutely, yes. I've never wanted to do anything more. And it's odd, but I don't just want to come for myself. I want to come for him, to please him. "Yes." I nod to him. "Yes," I repeat again.

His thumb presses against my clit, swirling in circles at the same pace he slides in and out of me. My breath catches in my chest as I squeeze the frame of the bed harder. It's almost too much. Almost. My body is riding the line somewhere between heaven and hell, suspended in some kind of naughty purgatory.

His pace quickens as he drops one leg from his shoulders, then the other. I instinctively wrap them around him, pulling him into me. Hanson's breathing becomes ragged as small groans escape him. God, he's so fucking hot.

"Let go," he says.

So that's exactly what I do. I don't break eye contact with him as he brings my body to the edge and pushes it over. Blinding fireworks are all I can see for the next several seconds as my body shudders and flails like it's trying to rip itself apart from the inside.

I collapse further into the mattress, my muscles no longer tense or rigid. I'm melted ice cream on a hot sidewalk. A pile of feathers you could blow into the wind with a single puff.

"You can't rest yet, love," he says. "I'm not done."

Using my legs as leverage, he flips me to one side, rolling me over to my stomach as he pulls me to my knees. He gently pushes my head against the bed and brings my arms behind me, holding them against the small of my back.

It's such a quick transition, seamless and commanding. Hanson has a way of being politely dominant if such a thing exists.

He rubs his dick against me, from my clit all the way back. Then he's inside me, thrusting so hard he grips my hands tighter to keep me in place.

The gentle moans are gone from me, replaced with guttural screams as he uses me for his pleasure. I'm thankful for this gag, for his forethought. And I want him to come. I want it bad.

After several more thrusts, I get what I want. Hanson's body crashes against mine, his body shaking as he squeezes my hands.

"Fuck," he says, the expletive slipping from his mouth as he exhales.

He collapses against me as I slide my knees down, my hands free to roam. Then, he rolls to his side, pulling me with him. In an instant, I'm the little spoon, our naked bodies twisted together as he holds me close.

Both of us lie still, gripping one another tightly and panting to catch our breaths. I'm exhausted and charged at the same time, my body letting me know it could fall asleep or do that again.

"Are you okay?" Hanson asks, his mouth close to my ear. His breath tickles my skin.

"I'm fantastic," I say, laughing. "You?"

"I'm wonderful, goddess," he says.

"No, say it your way," I say.

"I'm wonderful, *deusa*," he says. I can sense his smile as he speaks, causing me to smile.

After a few more minutes, we sit up to collect ourselves. I'm trying to figure out what should happen now. Is he going to leave? Should I ask him to stay?

I guess the first thing I should do is decide what I actually want to happen. It's been a while since I've been in this position. I don't want to be presumptuous either way. But when I put some thought to it, I want Hanson to stay. No part of me wants to go to bed alone after that.

Across the room, Hanson deposits the condom into the trash before turning toward me. His hands rest casually on his hips.

"Do you mind if I clean up?" he asks. "You could join me."

"You drive a hard bargain," I say, laughing.

We step into the shower just long enough to wash our bodies off, both of us giving most of our attention to sexy time body parts. After we towel off, I slip on a clean pair of panties and a tank top.

He slips the boxers he was wearing earlier back on and I take a long moment to appreciate his form. From his muscular legs to his toned torso, all the way up to his beautiful face, this man is perfection.

The ink over his chest is intricate and colorful, somehow accentuating the natural curves and cuts of his body. I didn't notice before, probably because I was blinded by pleasure, but both of his nipples are pierced. I've never really been into men with piercings but upon looking at them, I'm oddly turned on.

"So," he says, pausing. "What now?"

I know he's asking because ultimately it's up to me. He didn't automatically begin putting the rest of his clothes on or telling me he was leaving, which must mean he wants to stay. But he's not going to invite himself to do so either. Right? That must be what it means.

"Well, um," I say, hesitating. "I'd like you to stay if you want?"

Hanson smiles so wide that it looks like his face might split open. My cheeks grow warm as I reciprocate.

"Would it alarm you if I said I put a bag with a change of clothes in the back of my car just in case?" he asks.

"Would it alarm you if I said I changed my bedding earlier today just in case?" I ask.

Hanson closes the distance between us, placing one hand on either side of my face as he rubs the pad of his thumb over my bottom lip. He leans in, pressing his mouth to mine for a long, deep kiss before disappearing to get his bag.

While he's gone, I turn down the blankets and re-fluff the pillows as I try to remember the last time I slept in the same bed with a man. I never spent the night with the last guy I slept with. He always had an excuse regarding his schedule, early morning or needing to feed his pets or some other crap. Needless to say, it was short-lived.

Hanson returns quickly, replacing his boxers with clean ones. This pair is dark red and looks incredibly soft. Hanson looks good in this color, very, very good.

"What side of the bed do you sleep on?" he asks.

Shaking thoughts of what other colors he'd look good in, it takes me a moment to realize he's asking me something I need to respond to. "The left. If that's okay with you."

"It's your bed, love. I'm the guest," he says. "I'm adaptable."

Crawling beneath the blanket, I double-check that my alarm is set in the morning. "What time do you need to be up?"

"I have to pick up Ava by eight," he says. "Do you want to come with me?"

"To pick up Ava?" I ask.

"Yeah," he says. "I have to take her to school. The same place you're going."

I laugh. "Right, I know. I just didn't know if you'd want me going to where you work and stuff. Won't people be there?"

Hanson furrows his brows. "Um, well, probably only Will, but what does that matter?"

"I just didn't know if you'd want me to meet your friends and coworkers, that's all," I say.

Hanson's lips press into a sad line. He brings his fingertips to my jawline, caressing my skin with small, circular movements.

"Why wouldn't I want you to meet my friends?" he asks. "Who did this to you?"

My gaze falls away, breaking eye contact. It's the only response I can manage.

"Don't do that," he says. "Look at me."

I bite my bottom lip as I meet his eyes again, unsure what to say. "I told you I'm not very good at this."

"Listen," he says. "You're beautiful, smart, and funny. And you're a great mom. And you're worthy of so much more than you've been given. So yeah, come with me. Come by anytime. Let me hold your hand high in the air and declare to everyone I slept with you."

I laugh, unable to keep a straight face in the midst of his little speech. "You're silly."

"Maybe," he says. "But I mean it."

I kiss him hard, my forehead coming to rest against his. "Thank you."

"Now roll over so I can spoon you," he says. "And don't judge me if I grind against your ass a little."

I laugh again as I settle into his arms. "I wouldn't have it any other way."

As I attempt to fall asleep, the evening's events play over in my head. My body flushes at the newly formed memories of his hands on my body. I think about the date as a whole, and how wonderful Hanson is in his entirety.

It's going great until a little devil on my shoulder whispers math into my ear. Eight years is a long time. When I was giving birth to my son at twenty-two, Hanson was fourteen. Fourteen! Jesus. From twenty-five to now, my life was incredibly different than his. I did an immense amount of growing up. Which calls into question if he will be doing the same.

I guess it comes down to whether I think our age gap works in our favor or if it will ultimately be a source of friction, a demise. Maybe I'm getting ahead of myself, but that's what mothers do. We're always three steps ahead because most of our decisions are rooted in whether or not it's what's best for our children.

For once, though, I'd love to throw caution in the trash and do exactly what I want to do. And at the moment, that means falling asleep next to Hanson.

## TWO BIRDS

### HANSON

Call me crazy, but this morning the sky is as blue and bright as it's ever been. The birds are flying overhead, chirping happily. And freshly cut grass is all I can smell all the way to the shop.

As we drive over, I hold Thea's hand in an attempt to keep her calm. But she still uses the free one to straighten her collar and necklace and hair over and over again.

And to think, I thought I'd be the one who was nervous about the prospect of her meeting any one of my friends. But Will is good about meeting new people. Plus, she's a woman so maybe that will help.

Except, the moment we pull up to the shop, there are more vehicles than expected. I don't want to alarm Thea, so I play it as cool as I can, giving no hints as to the unexpected additions.

"Okay," I say. "Let's go get Ava."

The familiar ding of the bell sounds overhead as we walk

in, causing four heads to turn in our direction. Thea's hand grips mine harder as if to silently trigger an alarm. I squeeze back, reassuringly.

"*Olá*," I call out. "What's everyone doing here?"

Will steps around the counter, craning her neck.

"Oh hey," she says. "Jericho came in early to help me with something. Derek is here because it's his day off and thought he'd take care of Knox today. And Hawk is just checking in before he goes to his mom's house to help Drew."

Nearly everyone is here on the one day it would've been fine for them not to be. I can't help but laugh, because of course it would be this morning.

"And who's this?" Derek asks, looking toward Thea.

"That's Miss James," Ava says, interjecting from the hallway.

She runs over, not stopping until she's right in front of the two of us.

"Good morning, Ava," Thea says. "And hello to all of you as well."

She waves to the adults in the room, likely doing her best to hold it together being the center of attention.

"Did you guys have a sleepover?" Ava asks.

From across the room, Hawk chokes on his coffee.

"I'm sorry," he says. "Ava, that's not appropriate."

"Oh," Ava says. "Sorry. Hawk says I have no filter."

I press my lips together to keep myself from laughing, which probably wouldn't make the situation better.

"Thea, would you like a cup of coffee?" Will asks.

"Uh, yes, that would be lovely," Thea says, loosening her grip on my hand to follow Will to the coffee maker.

I walk toward the counter where all the guys have gathered, unable to wipe the smile from my face.

"So I take it the date went well?" Hawk asks.

"Yes," I say, proudly. "But that's all you're getting from me."

A few moments later, Thea walks toward me with two cups of coffee, handing me one. I hadn't asked for one, so it's as much a surprise as it is a much-needed treat.

I lean in close to her, pressing my lips to her ear. "*Obrigado, deusa.*"

"You're welcome," she says, kissing my cheek.

"How do you know what I said?" I ask.

"Lucky guess based on context clues," she says, winking.

"Okay, you two," Derek says. "Enough of whatever is happening that's making her turn pink."

Thea cups her hand over her face, presumably to shield eyes from seeing the aforementioned pink shade of her skin.

"Should we go?" I ask. "I feel like we should go."

Ava runs to grab her backpack from a chair, meeting us at the door. She pauses as we exit, causing us to stop just outside the shop.

"What's wrong?" I ask.

"Well, I usually walk next to you on this side of the sidewalk," she says, pointing to the inside. "But Miss James is there, so I'm just trying to figure out where to go."

"Oh, honey, I'm sorry," Thea says. "Would you like to walk in the middle?" Thea releases my hand, allowing for a space big enough for Ava to fit.

"No, no," Ava says. "You two hold hands. I can walk on the other side of you."

"Are you sure?" Thea asks.

"Yeah," Ava says. "It's fine."

We continue on like that, me holding Thea's hand with Ava on her other side. The three of us walk in unison toward the school. To an outsider, maybe we look like a family. This is a little crazy for me to think about, considering I've often felt I'd never have one of my own.

Sure, Bird's Eye is home, my home. Those people are my family. But I guess I mean "family" the way Hawk has formed one of his own. Or the way Avery has gone off in pursuit of his own. Or the way I secretly know that Derek carries a ring in his pocket, waiting for the right moment to ask Will to make one with him.

We make it to the school in time to see Shane pull into the parking lot with Ethan. He parks his car abruptly in the nearest spot, getting out in a huff.

Ethan steps out of the backseat, strapping his backpack on as he waves to Ava.

"What's this?" Shane asks, motioning to me. Oh god. Here we go.

Thea holds my hand tighter, and I don't know if that's for her benefit or mine.

"What are you talking about?" Thea asks.

Shane walks toward us in the same huffy way he parked, leaving Ethan to trail behind him. It's a fucking parking lot, dude. Watch out for your kid. It's what I want to say but don't. I bite my tongue hard as Thea looks past Shane to her son.

"Are you dating this guy?" Shane asks, looking me up and down.

"Hey, man," I say, putting my hand out. He doesn't take it like he did the other day which leads me to believe the difference between liking me and not liking me rests on whether or not I'm fucking his ex.

"Shane, stop it," Thea says. "There are kids present."

"Just tell me," Shane says.

"If you must know, yes," she says. "Not that it's your business."

"If someone is going to be around Ethan, it's my business," he says, crossing his arms over his chest.

"Ethan, how about you and Ava head inside?" Thea says.

The kids have been staring at the three of us, their necks craning, eyes wide. I'm relieved when she asks them to go in because I was about to. They don't need to hear any of this.

Once they're out of earshot, Thea's demeanor changes.

"Listen, Shane. I don't complain about the number of women you have had around Ethan in the past. I don't complain about the fact that you don't always get him when you're supposed to or bail at the last minute. I haven't dated anyone in years, and I haven't brought anyone around Ethan for even longer than that. So when I stand here and tell you right here and now that you absolutely will not try to sabotage my love life with this bullshit, I mean it," she says.

I don't even think she took a breath during that small speech. Honestly, I was just trying to keep a straight face the entire time. Literally no one, least of all Thea, needs me stepping in to say anything. This is her battle to fight out with her ex, and even though it's centered around my presence, it actually has very little to do with me.

Thea reaches for my hand, lacing her fingers with mine as she pulls me closer to her. It's a gesture that tells Shane she's not bullshitting and she's not backing down.

"Now, if you'd like to start over, Shane, this is Hanson. I believe you met the other day. And Shane, we're seeing each other," she says.

Everyone is silent for a moment. Shane looks from Thea's face to mine, then down to our joined hands and back to Thea's face again.

"Whatever," he says. "I have to get to work."

He gets back into his car and drives off in a huff, clearly unhappy with the outcome of the last several minutes.

Thea turns to me, shaking her head in what seems to be disbelief.

"I'm so sorry," she says. "He's such an asshole. God, I'm sorry."

"Don't be sorry," I say, pulling her body against mine. "It's okay, it's fine." I squeeze my arms around her, caressing her back in an attempt to calm her down. I hate that she feels like this when she has to go to work.

"He's so difficult for no reason," she says.

"Well, it's no surprise to me. And probably not to you either. But it doesn't matter. It doesn't change anything." I kiss her forehead, then her cheek, and finally her mouth.

Her hands grip the back of my T-shirt as the full force of her returned kiss does a good job of rendering me momentarily breathless.

"I'll pick you up after work and drive you home, since your car is at home," I say. "Maybe the kids can get a little tutoring session in at your place?"

"Yeah, that sounds good," she says.

After we say our goodbyes, I watch her walk into the school. At the last moment, she turns back, flashing me a smile. Damn, that woman.

# HARD TO FORGET

## THEA

Do you know what makes mundane daily life way more enjoyable? Do you know what instantly helps you shrug off a fight with your ex in your workplace parking lot? When you spent the night before having the best sex of your existence.

Today, I did the same math problem on the board pretty much all day. Every class seemed to have an issue with that same one. During lunch, I was reminded again about volunteering at the school dance in a couple of weeks. Plus, I have to dress up for it. Plus, I have to find five additional parent volunteers.

But none of that mattered. Not even a little. All I could think about all day was Hanson and what can only be described as his masterful sex skills. I didn't even think someone almost ten years younger could have that kind of talent for pleasure.

For a moment, it called into question how much practice

he's had, how many women have experienced that side of him. But ultimately I decided I couldn't care less. It's none of my business what he did before me.

The bell rings at school dismissal, drawing me back to reality. As I begin to gather my things, there's a delicious pang in my belly fueled by the fact that I know he's waiting outside for me.

"Ready to go, Mom?" Ethan asks from the door. As always, he's right on time.

"I sure am," I say. "And guess what?"

"What?" he asks.

"Ava is coming over," I say. "Along with Hanson. Is that okay?"

"Awesome," he says. "Yeah, of course, it's okay. Maybe we can order some pizza?"

"I think that's a great idea," I say.

We meet up with Ava in the hallway and all walk out together. She's equally excited about the plan once I fill her in as the two kids bound ahead of me, eager to get going.

Outside, we spot Hanson leaning against his car a few yards off. A wave of heat runs down my spine as I take in his form. Ripped black jeans and a tight black v-neck T-shirt don't sound impressive, but on Hanson, they're a weapon. His dark hair is pulled back into a knot but a few wild strands hang loose.

Then, he smiles. From across the parking lot, past everyone, to me. That grin is for me. And I feel it all the way down in my toes.

"*Olá*," he says. "How was everyone's day?"

He leans in and presses a small kiss to my cheek. There's nothing especially romantic about it, and I imagine he's reserving physical affection for after I speak to Ethan about the progress of events. I mean, it's only been one date, but the build-up to it makes it feel a little longer.

"Hey, Hanson," Ethan says. "Mom says we're ordering pizza!"

"Fantastic," Hanson says as he opens the car door for me.

My cheeks warm under his intense gaze as I slip past him to get in. The kids are occupied with their seatbelts, giving us a split-second moment of heated tension before returning to normal. A few more moments like this, and I'll be trying to figure out how to slip into the hallway closet for seven blissful minutes of heaven. If heaven had a sex dungeon.

As we pull up to my house, I take a moment to appreciate how blissfully normal this feels. Arriving home from work, not alone, with kids in the back, a man holding my hand. Honestly, it felt like this kind of thing might never happen.

It's not like I'm planning a wedding in my head or even assuming this will last longer than a few casual dates. But the experience is showing me that some kind of future is possible, and I've needed that for a while.

Inside, everyone piles their shoes by the door before Ethan tugs Ava to the table where they put their backpacks. Then, he asks if he can show her his room before they start as they slip off down the hallway.

My eyes find Hanson's across the room, both of us wearing a knowing smile. He closes the distance between us as my arms open to embrace him. The next thing I know, his hands are tangled into my hair, one of my legs is hitched up around his hip, and we're making out like two frenzied teenagers who only have a few minutes before their parents get home.

"I thought about you all day," he whispers into the sensitive skin beneath my ear, kissing and nibbling as I throw my head back.

"What did you think about?" I ask, exhaling deeply.

"This," he says, slipping one hand down to cup my breast. "And this." His hand trails down my stomach. "And this." He cups between my legs over my pants and a moan threatens to escape me.

We both hear the click of Ethan's door opening and separate in an instant. Making every attempt to smooth down my hair, Hanson reaches for his phone.

"I'll order the pizza," he says. "What does everyone want?"

I bury my face deep into the open cabinet, pretending to look for cups as the kids tell him what they want on their pizza. There's no escape from their curious eyes if I move from my position. I simply have to pray my skin isn't as red as my hair.

After the pizza is ordered, the kids sit at the table to go over some math problems while they wait for it to arrive. Hanson and I take a seat in the living room to talk while we wait.

I can't explain it, but these simple acts make me feel warm inside. It feels good to have people around. For a long time, it's just been me and Ethan. Don't get me wrong, I love him and our dynamic but it's easy to wish for more.

After a few minutes, the pizza arrives and we all gather

around the table to eat together. For the first time in a while, the table is full. There's talking and laughing, goofy faces, and second helpings.

If I'm being honest, I think Ethan needs this even more than I do. There's limited family to speak of on my side. And as for Shane, his family is as reliable as he is. He didn't fall far from the tree at all.

And I don't care what anyone says. You're not meant to be alone or live in near isolation. Connections are important, mental, physical, and emotional.

After dinner, it's time for Hanson and Ava to leave and I'm filled with a sort of sadness that the evening has to come to an end.

Ethan and Ava hug goodbye, saying they'll see each other tomorrow. Hanson wraps his arms around me, and I return the gesture, squeezing him tightly.

"Goodnight, *deusa*," he whispers, kissing me on the cheek.

"I'll text you later," I say, blushing.

Ethan and I wave from the door as they drive off, and then he turns to me.

"I need your help, Mom," he says.

"What's up, buddy?" I ask.

"Can you help me figure out how to ask Ava to the school dance?" he asks.

My heart skips a hundred beats in an instant. My son, my Ethan, likes a girl. He's going to a dance. He's going to ask her out. As a mother, I'm both shocked and elated.

Ava is a good girl, smart and kind. As far as potential first girlfriends go, I couldn't ask for better.

After assuring Ethan I'd help him figure it out, we settle down for the evening. He disappears to his room, likely to get in a little video game time before bed.

As I pull out my phone to text Hanson, I'm overwhelmed with how different life feels today compared to just a week ago.

Maybe there's hope for me yet.

# TRULY MADLY DEEPLY
## THEA

Over the past week, I've seen Hanson every day. And not just when he picks Ava up from school. He's come over for dinner several times, taken both me and Ethan out for ice cream, and, over the weekend, we all went to the zoo.

He was around so much that I had to sit down with Ethan and have a serious talk about how he felt about it. Making sure he's comfortable is high on my priority list. But to my surprise and relief, he was perfectly happy and let me know he likes Hanson. He even went so far as to say he approves. And believe it or not, his approval is necessary.

Halfway through the day, Hanson texted me asking if we wanted to go to a little get-together this evening. At first, I told him Ethan would be with his dad. But no sooner than I texted that, I received a text from Shane. As if he has psychic powers, he canceled getting Ethan.

Part of me didn't care, because that meant he could go with me and hang out with Ava. But mostly I'm frustrated because it was going to be a night alone with Hanson. He hasn't spent the night at all as we agreed it was too soon to do in front of Ethan.

Which means another night of no cuddles or sex. Do you know what it's like to have the best sex of your life and then not have an opportunity for a repeat performance? Shane is probably doing this shit on purpose.

The bell rings for the end of the day, and I turn my thoughts to the plan we've devised. Earlier today, I asked Ava to stop by my classroom now. And instead of coming to meet me, Ethan is to run outside and meet up with Hanson.

Thirty seconds later, Ava is at my door and step one is complete. I take another minute or two to gather my things, giving Ethan and Hanson time to get set up.

"Walk out with me," I say to Ava. "How was your day?" I make every attempt to distract her so she doesn't think this is weird or ask where Ethan is. And thankfully, she plays right into it, telling me about her other classes.

Once outside, I scan to find Hanson and Ethan exactly where they're supposed to be. Ethan has retrieved the sign from my car and Hanson is holding the flowers and chocolates.

"What's going on?" Ava asks as we step closer.

"Ava," Ethan says, projecting his voice confidently. "Will you go to the school dance with me?"

His words mimic what's written on the sign in bright

lettering. Though, all I can see is the smile plastered across his face. It overwhelms me to see my baby boy like this. I couldn't be more proud.

"Yes," Ava says. "Of course, I will go to the dance with you."

There's a slight relief in me as she gives her answer. Truth be told, I was holding my breath for him. Based on what Hanson told me, I was pretty sure what she would say but I still had a moment of panic.

Ethan puts down his sign, grabbing the flowers and box from Hanson to give to her.

"Good job, my man," Hanson says to Ethan in hushed tones.

As the kids hug and talk, I step closer to Hanson. "That went well."

"Yes," he says. "But there's one more thing."

"What's that?" I ask.

Hanson walks to the tree just behind him, retrieving the second bouquet and box of chocolates.

"I know these don't hold a candle to the first ones I got you, but I didn't want to be empty-handed," he says. "Will you go to the dance with me?"

A smile spreads across my face, the kind accompanied by brimming tears. It's the unexpectedness of it for me, the total surprise and thoughtfulness behind it.

"Of course," I say. "I'd love to go to the dance with you."

Upon my answer, Ava and Ethan begin clapping as Hanson embraces me, hands still full. I bask in the moment, allowing myself to be present and happy. Sometimes I have intrusive thoughts about what it all means and the future and compare it to my past. But not right now. Right now, I just exist.

We part ways after I fill Hanson in on Shane and how Ethan will be attending with me now. When we arrive home, Ethan makes a mad dash to his room saying he needs to look awesome for the party. Which causes me to scurry to my room because I can't show up bested by my son.

I hadn't put much thought into what to wear, but now I'm second-guessing my casual approach. Shoving jeans back into the drawer, I reach for a simple cocktail dress. It's nothing super fancy—black and knee length with thin straps. I throw on some accompanying gold jewelry and retouch my makeup, giving my eyes a smokier evening look.

"Mom, are you ready?" Ethan calls from the living room. "Hurry up, we can't be late."

I've never known my son to be this excited to go anywhere. It's usually me calling for him, dragging him out the door to social events. He wasn't even interested in going to the school dance before he became closer to Ava. Which tells me this is important to him.

"I'm coming," I say, grabbing my purse as I make my way to the front door.

"Wow, Mom," Ethan says, his eyebrows shooting up on his forehead. "You look beautiful."

"Thank you, son," I say, smiling.

As we get into the car, I can't help but recognize how happy I am. Ethan is happy, doing better in math, and has a freakin' date. We both have the start of what seems to be a pretty great social life. And let's not forget, I'm horny again. I was starting to think I was broken but Hanson has certainly shown me the way.

---

Following Hanson's instructions, we park behind the tattoo shop where I find he's waiting for us.

"*Olá,*" he says as I exit the car. "You look beautiful, *deusa.*"

"Thank you," I say, blushing.

"Ready to meet the extended gang?" he asks.

I nod, suddenly nervous at the prospect of meeting everyone for an extended period. Even though this isn't high school, I can't help but hope they like me. Given what I know about all of them, being accepted into their circle is a big deal. I'm sure it means a lot to Hanson, which is only added pressure.

Hanson opens the door as we all step inside. Scanning the room, I realize there are even more people here than I expected. Some I recognize, others are new to me. But I'm relieved to see I made the right choice in changing my outfit. Everyone seems similarly dressed for a cocktail hour.

Drew waves to me from across the room. I wave back, glad to see her here. I know the situation with Hawk's mother must be difficult.

Hanson's hand slides to my lower back as he guides me around for introductions. Each time he tells someone who I am, he makes sure to introduce Ethan with equal importance. It's something I hadn't considered, but in seeing him do it, I can't help but mark its significance.

"There y'all are," Will says as she leans in to give me a quick hug. "I'm so glad you could come."

"Thank you for having us," I say.

"Oh, don't thank me," she says. "I have no idea why we're getting together. This was all Hawk's idea."

"Mom," Ethan cuts in. "I need to go to the bathroom."

"Hanson, why don't you show him where it is and get us all some drinks?" Will says. "I'll keep Thea company."

Hanson kisses me on the cheek before giving Will a look as if to warn her. I'm sure it's one of those "Don't say anything stupid" looks. I'm familiar with them.

After he disappears with Ethan, Will turns to me sporting a mischievous grin.

"So," she says. "Tell me how it's going."

"Um, I think it's going well," I say. "He's been nothing but wonderful. He's thoughtful and attentive. All things I'm not used to at all." I laugh, thinking about how true those words are.

"So your ex was pretty terrible, huh?" she asks.

"That's putting it mildly," I say. "He was incredibly selfish."

"Well, Hanson is a good one," she says. "Even if he is a little emotionally stunted."

Her words take me by surprise. "What do you mean?"

"Oh nothing, really," she says. "It's just that he doesn't

talk about himself beyond a certain point. And I'm sure you know by now, he doesn't talk about his past at all."

"Right." I don't know what else to say beyond that. It's still early between us so maybe I haven't exactly seen this side of him yet. But it worries me nonetheless.

"Don't worry," she says as if she's reading my mind. "I'm sure it'll be different with you. He seems to like you very much."

Her words do the exact opposite of calming me. Now my mind is spiraling down a path of uncertainty. What if it's no different with me? How will I know? How long would I need to wait to see if it's different? Timelines for these types of situations aren't exactly written out in a manual somewhere. Although the older I get the more I think everyone should have one.

Will shifts gears, turning to walk me toward other people. Jericho introduces me to his wife Kate, who's an absolute doll. They've been married longer than anyone here, which means they tied the knot pretty young.

Avery and Helena are also here, up visiting from Nashville. I recall being told he'd moved to be with her not all that long ago. They're in town specifically for this little party, which has me wondering about its significance. It doesn't seem like people would be dressed up and coming from out of town unless there was a plot afoot.

As we circle back to Hanson, he hands us both drinks.

"Ethan is on the balcony with Ava," he says, pointing toward the open sliding door.

"If I could have everyone's attention, please," Hawk says, clinking a butter knife against his raised glass.

I knew it. Something is afoot. Everyone begins to gather around him in a circle. He's chosen a pretty central space to stand, which makes me think he's about to announce something pretty important.

As quickly as he stepped into the spotlight, Hawk steps aside as his brother Derek comes to the center. Oh god.

"Will," he says, holding his hand out.

I watch her as she looks from side to side like she's not herself. Oh god. I think I know what's about to happen. Turning to Hanson, he smiles as he squeezes my hand. He knew about this all along, didn't he?

Slowly, Will steps forward, taking Derek's outstretched hand. She leans in toward him, whispering something out of earshot to everyone else. If I had to guess, it's something like, "What the hell is going on?"

"Will, these past months with you have been nothing short of spectacular. I will never be able to tell you how amazed I am. The person you are, the person you make me. I'll never be able to thank you enough for how you moved and accepted Connor, how good you are with him."

Derek dips down, his hand traveling into his pocket. With his knee planted firmly on the floor, he presents a small box to her.

"Willette Susan Archer," he says. "Will you make me the happiest man alive and be my wife?"

Will's had her hand over her mouth since Derek began dropping to one knee. But the instant he finishes speaking, her hand drops to reveal the biggest smile. Tears fall over her cheeks.

"Yes," she says. "Of course, yes."

Derek pushes the diamond ring onto her finger as the two embrace. They hug and kiss as we all cheer. I feel so fortunate to be part of such a special, intimate moment.

"Thank you for bringing me," I whisper to Hanson.

"Thank you for coming," he says just before kissing my lips.

The rest of the evening is laughing and dancing, drinking, and exchanging stories about each other. Hanson laughs harder than I've ever seen him. Ethan and Ava are on the couch playing games with Connor. The happiness in this room is thick and palpable.

As everything winds down, people begin to leave. The kids start looking tired and it's time to go. Hanson walks us to my car where Ethan wastes no time climbing into the back. He'll likely fall asleep before we even get home.

"I had a great time," I say.

"Me too," he says. "It's a shame it has to end."

My head twists toward the back seat of my car where Ethan is already very much asleep. "Well, it doesn't have to."

Hanson raises his eyebrows. "What do you mean?"

"As long as you're gone before he wakes up, I think I'd like you to stay over," I say.

"That can be arranged," he says, running his hand over the scruff on his jaw. "Let me run home for clothes and I'll be right over."

"Deal," I say, leaning in to kiss him one last time before we part.

He brushes the pad of his thumb over my lips, then turns away. Goosebumps run down my back and everything tingles as I get behind the wheel of my car.

This man. This man is fire. And I want to burn myself alive.

## ALL EYES ON YOU
### HANSON

Stopping at home to change out of my fancy clothes and grab an overnight bag takes me no time at all. And when I arrive at Thea's place, she's already put Ethan to bed, changed into pajamas, and poured us both wine. I guess we get points for being an efficient couple. Er, if a couple is what we are.

"I can't believe I got to watch Will and Derek get engaged," she says. "It was so amazing."

I take a sip of wine from my glass. "Yeah, it was pretty great. And about time." I laugh, thinking about the past year when things took off between them. For Will, I imagine she's dreamt about this day since they were kids. It fills me with happiness for both of them.

"Do you ever think about stuff like that?" Thea asks.

"Like what? Getting married?" I shift positions on the couch to face her a bit more.

"Yeah," she says. "Getting married, or having kids, or even just living with someone."

"Sure," I say. "I mean, I've thought about it once or twice, I guess." A part of me doesn't want to say that I've only really thought about it since meeting her. That seems a little creepy.

"What would you say we're doing now?" she asks before taking a sip of her wine.

I smirk. "Well, when people ask, I tell them we're dating. They ask if you're my girlfriend, and I'd like to tell them that you are." My hand reaches across to tuck a loose strand of hair behind her ear.

Before either of us say anything else, she slides forward, her mouth connecting with mine. Her tongue laps against mine as my hands pull her on top of my lap to straddle me. I dig my fingertips into the soft flesh of her hips and ass. Her hands thread my hair, tugging at it as she grips the back of my neck.

Thea's scent is intoxicating. I inhale and taste, inhale and taste, over and over again. I don't think I will ever tire of kissing her. She's mentioned her inexperience a couple of times, but I've yet to find a single thing she's bad at. Thea is the perfect mix of tenderness and ferocity.

She pulls back from our kiss, staring down at my face for a long time. I stare right back at her, hoping she sees all of me.

"You know," she says as she slides off my lap. "Before I can officially agree to be your girlfriend, I need the answers to some questions."

Her mischievous grin doesn't have me worried. "Ask

away." I settle back into the couch with my glass of wine as she straightens her shorts.

"What's your zodiac sign?" she asks.

"Oh god, you're not one of those people who believe in that stuff, are you?" I ask, rolling my eyes.

"Just tell me," she says, laughing.

"Fine," I say. "I'm a Virgo. And I only know that because of an ex."

"And what's your favorite color?" she asks.

"Green," I say, sipping my wine.

"And your favorite animal?" she asks.

"Lions." As I say this, my hand begins to slide from its resting place on her knee upward over her thigh.

"Tell me what happened with your father," she says. It's not even a question, but more a statement. If I didn't know better, it sounds like a demand for information.

My hand recoils from her leg, balling into a fist. It's not out of anger toward her, but more a reflexive reaction. Everything about me recoils at the thought of him.

"I don't want to talk about that," I say.

"But-" she says.

I cut her off. "I said I don't want to talk about that," I say more firmly.

"Don't you think if we're going to be together, you should be able to talk to me about it?" she asks, sliding her hand to find my balled fist, coaxing it open.

"Why?" I let her take my hand. "It doesn't matter."

"It does matter," she says. "It's a very large part of your past and I think it's hurting you."

"You have no idea what hurt is," I say. Before I know it, I'm on my feet, retrieving my bag, and sliding on my shoes at the door.

"Wait, what are you doing?" she says. "Don't go."

"I think it's best if I do," I say. "I don't want to say anything else I'll regret later."

"See, this is what I'm talking about," she says. "This isn't good."

"You're right," I say, opening the door. "I'm not good." I exit, shutting the door behind me before either of us can say anything else.

I knew something like this was going to happen. They always push and push and want more. Can't someone just accept what I'm willing to give and let that be enough? Why does everyone want to unpack the trauma of my past like it's some goddamn present wrapped in a bow?

Why can't I be enough?

## NO REASON

### THEA

It's Monday afternoon and I could let it be the fifth day Hanson avoids me. I wouldn't say he's ignoring me altogether. But since trying to speak to him about his father, he's picked Ava up from school with nothing more than a cursory hug and kiss and barely responded to texts. Over the weekend, he claimed to be busy but I don't believe that.

So, as I walk toward him now with Ava and Ethan by my side, I have a choice. Let this continue until, eventually, we're not talking at all. Or salvage it with what I consider to be subpar actions.

"Hey," I say once I'm close enough.

"Hi," he says.

"Can you please come over tonight? We need to talk," I say.

Hanson shifts from one foot to the other, hesitation written all over his face. He runs his hand along the back of his neck and I think he's about to avoid me again.

"I promise I will not bring up that one thing," I say, hoping to tilt the odds in my favor.

"What time?" he asks.

And I'm in. Sort of. "Seven?"

"Okay," he says.

A quick hug and kiss later, he's already walking away as Ethan and I head for my car. It's a start, right? Honestly, I don't have a clue what I'm going to say to him later, but I know this can't continue. If he wants to end things, it should be now. Although, that's not what I want.

———

Hanson arrives at seven on the dot. Out of desperation, I've not only allowed Ethan extra snacks and soda pop, but I'm letting him have them in his room while he watches a movie.

"Thank you for coming," I say, sitting down next to him on the couch.

"Of course," he says.

The tone of his voice isn't him at all. It's quiet and somber. Hanson's voice is usually warm and husky, his accent soothing and sensual. I hate this.

"Listen," I say, swallowing. "I'm sorry about that night. I never should've asked. I-"

Hanson holds up his hand, gently cutting me off.

"No," he says. "I'm sorry. I shouldn't have reacted that way. I wasn't very mature about it."

"We don't have to talk about him," I say. "Not until you want to. Or ever."

He runs his hands against the tops of his thighs, smoothing the ripples in the dark denim material.

"Okay," he says.

"Okay?" I ask. "Like everything is okay now and we can make out and stuff?" The last-ditch effort to lighten the mood works.

Hanson's smile grows and brightens as his hands reach for me.

"As in yes, we can make out," he says as he pulls me on top of him. "Because I have missed your mouth."

Our lips connect, mouths opening for each other. We're right back where we were the night everything went bad, but it won't this time. This time, it's all kissing and no talking. Of course, even as I'm presently engaged in the kissing, my mind wanders off. It's hard not to think this might always be how it is. What if we can never talk about it? Realistically speaking, that feels insane to me.

I'm not trying to be nosy just for the sake of being nosy. I feel like not sharing the dark parts of your past with someone you're involved with means you're sort of cutting the opportunity for a deep connection off at the knees. Surely that's not what he wants?

So many questions swirl around my head and my tongue swirls around his. But I have to push them aside if I want to enjoy what's happening now and what will be happening in a little while.

After we manage to pry ourselves apart, I go check on Ethan and get him ready for bed. Luckily once he lays down, he's pretty much instantly asleep and does so soundly. While

I'm taking care of him, Hanson slips into my bedroom to—in his words—get prepared. I don't know what that means but it makes me no less excited about it.

Maybe he's a little shut-off. Maybe he can't open up so well. But I'll tell you one thing. Hanson Serrano is fucking great in bed. His hands, his mouth, his dick—it doesn't matter what he's using. It's legendary. I'm surprised his name isn't written on every stall in every women's bathroom in this city.

*For life-altering sex, call this guy.*

## DANCE WITH MY DEMONS

### HANSON

Inside Thea's bedroom, I remove a bit of binding rope from my bag and place it at the foot of her bed. I take everything off except my black boxer briefs, and I wait. There's no getting comfortable or cozying into the blankets. No, this isn't soft. She wants to experience things, and make up for lost time. I believe her exact words were something about wishing she'd "slutted it up" more in her youth.

And let's not do that thing where we shame women for their sexual appetites. They can be as hungry and as devilish as they want to be. It's no one's business but their own.

Thea slips through the door, her eyes growing bigger as she scans my bare chest and lower.

"Is that a rope?" she asks, pointing down.

"Yes." My answer doesn't seem to scare her off as she continues to advance the room.

"Are you tying me up?" she asks, coming to stand toe to toe with me.

"That's the plan," I say. "That a problem?"

"No," she whispers, her voice softer now.

"Good." I reach for the bottom edge of her shirt, pulling it over her head and discarding it to the floor. Next, I finger the elastic band in her shorts and jerk them down along with her panties in one fluid motion.

"Turn around," I say.

Thea spins on her heels, allowing me to unclasp her bra—the last item to go. Wrapping my arms around her waist, I trail kisses down her spine and over her shoulder blades as she leans back into me.

"Get on the bed," I say as I bend to grab the rope.

Positioning her to the center, I spread her legs apart so that each is as close to the bottom posts of her bed as possible. Ever so gently, I wrap one end of the rope around her ankle and then around the post. I trail the rope to the other side and repeat the same thing to the other ankle.

"This way I can take my time with you," I say. "And you can't get away."

"What about my arms?" she asks.

"Well, I was going to let you use your hands this time, but if you insist?" I turn to find something to bind her.

"Wait," she says. "I want to use my hands."

"Good girl," I say. "Comfortable?"

"Yes," she whispers.

Looking at her like this, helpless against my advances, hungry for what I'm going to do to her—it makes me ache. It makes me throb.

I crawl up between her legs and lean down, blowing warm

breath against her sensitive skin. Just this small action sends her wiggling and attempting to arch toward me.

"Patience," I say.

"I have none when it comes to you," she says.

Leaning down further, I flatten my tongue and press it against her clit. With the way her legs are tied, everything is open to me and I'm taking full advantage. I run my tongue up and down over her until her knees wobble. Her hands are too busy holding a pillow over her face to stifle her noises to be concerned with trying to stop me. Which is exactly what I had predicted.

Quickening my pace, I aim to edge her—bring her right to the brink of orgasm and then stop. I lick and suck, even nibble until she begins to quiver. Then I pull away.

Thea exhales deeply like she's been holding her breath for far too long.

"I don't know if I love it or hate it when you do that," she says, clawing at the pillow.

My fingers gently trail over her inner thighs, her hips, and then the center of her. The key is to calm everything in her body down just enough to rev it up again.

I lower my head once more, her chest rising and falling slowly with each breath. Then, I go again. Full force. I suck on her clit as I glide two fingers inside her. She's so wet, the act is effortless. But it causes her to make the most delicious noises, even if they are muffled by a pillow.

Ruthless in my pursuit, I edge her twice more. It's the slowest, most deliberate torture but it's necessary.

"Please," she begs.

It's the only word she gets out and I know it's time. My mouth connects with her one last time, but I don't stop when she begins to quiver. Her knees begin to shake as she bucks and arches toward me against her constraints.

I lick and suck, relentlessly delving into her over and over again until her entire body tenses. She grips the pillow tightly against her face as she lets out a full scream. Thankfully, the pillow does its job in containing it pretty well. That definitely would've woken someone up.

There's no way to wipe the smile from my lips as I lean back to look down at her. As Thea finally uncovers her face, I bask in her hazy, wild orgasm glow. If you don't think women have a glow post-orgasm, you're not paying attention. It's the one moment when all their shields are down when nothing else exists outside of their pleasure. And it's beautiful.

I take care in untying her ankles, pushing the rope to the floor as I climb back onto the bed.

"Come here," she says, straddling one leg on either side of me.

Her hands find my jawline as she pulls me down for a kiss, tasting herself from my mouth. Inhaling her deeply, I wrap my arms beneath her and pull her in, cradling her to my chest.

"Make love to me," she whispers. "Look into my eyes and make love to me."

There's something in her eyes, a depth I can't explain. All I know is I could fall into them and drown. I've never made love to anyone before. I've done sex. I've done a lot of fucking. But I'd never describe anything I've done under the category of making love. This look she's giving me though…makes me want to try.

I kiss her again, parting her lips with my tongue slowly as her hands grip my back. There's an intoxicating quality about the way her feet hook around the back of my legs. Everything is heat and light as our bodies melt into one another. Unable to withstand another moment of this, I slide my dick into her.

Thea gasps, sinking her fingertips into my rigid shoulder blades. Her eyes grow wide before her whole face settles into a softness akin to being a little drunk or maybe after you've taken an edible. And I love it. I love that I can make her feel so good.

I push into her slowly over and over again. Maybe it's because I'm not used to this slow, intimate sort of thing, or maybe because it's her. God, maybe it's both. But making love to Thea like this, looking into her eyes…it's more than I can take. And I don't fight it when my orgasm erupts from me, causing my body to stiffen.

"Yes," she says, holding onto me. "Yes."

My face comes to rest on her tits as I collapse on top of her. I'm still careful not to crush her, though she grips me tightly like she'd be okay with it. Her fingertips trace delicate little circles over my spine as I attempt to catch my breath.

Then it dawns on me. "Oh god, I didn't have a condom on. I'm so sorry."

"It's okay," she says. "I knew you didn't. I wanted it that way."

"Do we need to do something?" I ask. "Like one of those pills? Whatever you need, I'll run and get it."

"Relax," she says, giggling. "I'm on birth control."

"Oh," I say. "Well just ignore me and let's return to the nice moment we were having before I panicked."

We both laugh as I roll off her. She immediately buries herself in the crook of my arm, resting her head on my chest. A few moments of comfortable silence pass as our breathing returns to normal.

"So should we take a quick shower or bask in our juices like a Thanksgiving turkey?" I ask.

Thea immediately cracks up laughing, her hand muffling the sound because this would be about the worst time to accidentally wake Ethan up.

"I can't believe you just said that," she says. "Come on. Let's shower."

"Hey," I say, holding up my hands. "I'm not above being a turkey."

A soft towel thuds against my head as I fail to evade Thea's toss.

"You know, I take that back. I wouldn't want to be a turkey," I say.

"Why not?" she asks.

"Because they only hook up once a year during mating season. And the female turkey only gets one partner," I say. "No thank you."

"One day you're going to have to tell me why you know so much about the mating habits of so many random animals," she says, laughing.

"I have a Master's Degree in animal science," I say. "The

mating habits and rituals were a particular interest of mine. I just found them intriguing."

"I'm sorry, what?" she asks. "When the hell did you do that?"

"I started earning college credits in high school. By the time I graduated, I was halfway to a Bachelor's," I say. "Now let's go shower." I kiss her lips and head into the bathroom.

Even though I was forced into explaining in further detail how I came about my degree, and why I'm not using it, all-in-all I would say it was a successful shower.

We got out, dried off, slipped into clean clothes, and even made out a little before spooning.

Now, the problem is, Thea's been asleep for twenty minutes and I'm still wide awake. My mind is a swirling vortex of too many questions and not enough answers—all of which are giving me major anxiety.

When I think about making love to her again, I'm strangely turned on and frightened. It feels serious. When I think about Ethan, and what I might be in his life, I think about my father and realize I probably don't have the skills to be worth a damn at step-parenting. And the fact that I'm taking all of this into consideration leaves me with one personally terrifying question I'm not even sure I want the answer to.

Am I falling in love with her?

## ONLY LOVE CAN HURT LIKE THIS
### THEA

Despite what I'd call a minor itch in my brain, I'm on cloud nine today. Last night with Hanson was nothing short of amazing. Honestly, every moment with him seems better than the last.

This morning was perfectly orchestrated. We successfully managed to sneak him out before Ethan woke up and even had time to steal a kiss or two at the door as we said goodbye.

And this itch in my brain? Well, I'd be lying if I said Hanson seemed normal. I detected subtle hints of something nagging at him as we drifted to sleep and again as we parted ways this morning. I can't put my finger on it but there was something off. I even asked if he was okay but he said he was fine. Maybe I should chalk it up to being early morning or a possibility that he's only slept over twice so he may still be getting comfortable.

"Miss James?" Teddy says, his hand raised high in the air.

"Yes, Teddy?" I ask, pulling myself from my thoughts.

"Aren't we supposed to be choosing partners for the next assignment now?" he asks.

The entire class is staring up at me like I've been frozen in place for a lot longer than I have. "Yes, thank you. Please do that now." Little brown noser. No one likes a kiss ass, Teddy.

Ava runs straight to Ethan, which is expected. I love watching them now. Their little romance is pretty adorable, even if it does pull at all my motherly heartstrings. Once everyone is paired up, I put the problem they have to work on the board.

I'm not going to lie. It's a doozy. This is why it's a partnership assignment. There are multiple steps and the worksheet required paragraphs of explanation as to why they solved it this way. It's supposed to keep them busy for the remainder of the class period.

My phone buzzes on my desk behind me as I finish explaining everything. As they get started, I take a seat and grab my phone.

**HANSON: I think we both know this was never going to last. It was only a matter of time before I disappointed you or you got tired of me not wanting to talk about certain things about myself. I should end it now before this results in more devastating pain. I know you're going to hate me for this and I'm sorry but I'm doing it to save you from me.**

I read the text over again, tears brimming my eyes. There's no choice but to excuse myself from the classroom, seeking solace in the empty hallway. Tears come in waves as sadness and anger fight for first place. What a coward. What a fucking cowardly way to end this.

By text? What the fuck? I don't even deserve the decency of a face-to-face explanation? Maybe it's the age gap. Maybe at his age, this is how things are done. But not mine. I deserve better than that.

It would have been better if he didn't say anything at all before sending a stupid fucking text. God, I hate technology. I hate its ability to strip down social interactions, making it easier for assholes to hide. The people like me, the ones who try to be decent humans are the ones who suffer.

What now? Dry my tears and walk back into class? Jesus, I'm going to be distracted by this all day and unable to focus on my feelings and processing this. But unlike some, that's what normal people fucking do.

Absent-mindedly, I run my hands down my sides, as if to straighten myself. Although, I'm not rumpled, so it's without purpose. Using the back of my hand, I wipe the tears from my cheeks and under my eyes. All I can do is attempt to return my face to a neutral state.

This is what happens for parents, in particular, the single ones and the ones in difficult relationships. We shoulder it. It isn't fair and we never really get to grieve or process anything that happens to us because we're too busy tending to someone else's needs. We shoulder it. And we always will.

As I return to the classroom, it appears everyone is still quite busy with their work. And today, that's more of a blessing than I can explain. My mind turns his text over and over as I'm left wondering if I should reply. What would I say?

**ME: You're a coward.**

I hit the back button and erase it, thinking better of the bluntness. Though, it's hard to contain at this point.

**ME: You couldn't at least tell me face-to-face like a man?**

Again, I hit the back button, this time because terms like "like a man" make me feel disgusting. Projecting gender on mannerisms is outdated.

**ME: I wish you'd reconsider.**

I stare at the words on my phone for a long while, wondering if I could be the type of woman who has to convince someone to be with her. But it's hard for me to think that's how it should be. I deserve a person who knows they want me, who won't run away.

**ME: Ok.**

I quickly hit send on the one-word reply so I can't change my mind. Ok. That's all he's getting from me. I'm not arguing. I'm not begging or pleading. I didn't do it with Shane and I'm not doing it now.

Sliding my phone into my desk drawer to avoid temptation, I return my full focus to the class of kids. I make my way down each aisle, checking in and helping where I can.

"Are you okay?" Ava asks as I come to her and Ethan.

"Of course, why do you ask?" I say.

"I don't know," she says. "Just a feeling, making sure."

"You're sweet," I say. "Thank you but everything is good."

The look in her eyes suggests she doesn't fully believe me.

Kids know too much and can sense too much. Adults don't give them enough credit.

The bell rings for their lunch break and I breathe a sigh of relief as they all file out. I just need five minutes to myself. Five minutes to hard reset and I'll be okay.

It's a lie I tell myself often.

## INSANE

### HANSON

The good Dr. Russell is running a few minutes late to our session today, which has given me too much quiet time with my thoughts. As I wait in the same chair I use every week, I'm suddenly aware of how lumpy the ass cushion is. I suppose he's usually here, distracting me from anything else that might take up space in my mind.

But today of all days, I'm here wishing I could hear the tapping of that goddamn pen already. He's never really been late before which leads me to believe this is some sort of penance for my behavior this past week. It's been like this from the moment I sent that god-awful text to Thea.

That day, I didn't tattoo a single person. I had a cancellation on an appointment that was supposed to take up most of my day. Then, it rained. And when I say it rained, I mean the sky opened up and God himself dumped buckets of water on the city. If I didn't know better, I'd say he was probably spitting on me specifically. So, there were no walk-ins either.

In the days following, I almost got ran over by a bike messenger, I spilled piping hot coffee down my leg approximately two minutes after I poured it, and I had to ask Will to pick up Ava for me which prompted a lot of questions and her punching me right in the gut, and I lost my favorite sunglasses. All in all, I'd say that's a pretty fucking terrible week.

But I deserved that punch. And the colorful names she spewed at me. What's fucked up is I know she did it all out of care and concern. To someone outside our circle, that probably seems ridiculous. But Will punched me with love.

"Sorry I'm late," Dr. Russell says as he shuts the door behind me and rounds my chair to get to his. "Let's dive right in. How was your week?"

"It's been pretty awful, actually," I say. "And I think it's karma."

"I'm sorry to hear you had a bad week but why do you think it's karma? Karma for what?" he asks.

"I broke things off with Thea," I say. "Honestly, it was for the best. It was only a matter of time before it ended anyway."

"Okay, I'm going to come back to that but let me get this straight. You think karma dealt you a bad week because you decided to end things with Thea?" he asks as he stares at me like I've said something insane.

"Yeah, pretty much." I nod. It's not a crazy thought. At least I didn't think it was until now.

"You thinking its karma would imply you did something wrong, like a bad thing," he says. "So elaborate."

"Well, I texted her-"

"I'm going to stop you right there," he says, holding up his hand. "You mean to tell me you texted her to end it?"

"I thought it would be easier than face-to-face," I say.

"Easier for who? You? Because it certainly doesn't make it easier for her," he says.

Dr. Russell leans back into his chair as he begins to tap his pen rapidly. And he's probably right. It was easier for me. If I'd tried to do it in person, I'd have backed out. And I needed to do it. I don't have to say this out loud, though. He already knows the answer.

"Can I be blunt with you?" he asks.

"Of course," I say.

"You fucked up," he says. "You fucked up big and now you're sitting here whining about your bad week like it's some divine bringer of justice that's got you down. But you know what I think?"

He pauses, clearly wanting an answer from me. In the past, Dr. Russell has occasionally given me some hard truths. And I have a feeling this is one of those times as well. "Yeah."

"I think you got scared. I think the idea of having to open up to someone has you spooked, and instead of facing it, you're running away. And I think you know you fucked up. As a result, your head hasn't been right since. You're not in the game, you're not focused. And the results are some misfortunes. And they're all your fault," he says, breathless as he finishes.

He never gets like this unless he's passionate about what he's saying, so I know it means something to him to be saying all of this to me. His words gnaw at my insides less like an undetected parasite and more like a brown bear ripped me open and shoved its face inside.

We sit in silence for several long minutes. Dr. Russell makes a deliberate effort to tap his pen as hard as he can against his notepad. The rhythm is steady and projected. I honestly don't know what to say to him which is concerning to me. Normally, I want to talk to him and I have a lot to say outside of the topic of my father. I usually have no trouble drumming up something to continue our conversations. But not this time.

Perhaps this is stunned silence, the shock and awe of something I don't want to face in the least. And I can't believe I'm about to say what I'm about to say.

"Maybe you're right," I say.

"Come again?" he asks. He heard me. But he wants to hear it again.

"I said, maybe you're right. Maybe I am scared of her. So what? Maybe she frightens me for a lot of reasons. But I didn't want to hurt her. That's not why I did it. I did it to protect her," I say.

"Protect her from what?" he asks.

"From me, doc," I say sternly. "From me. From what I might be one day."

Dr. Russell's pen finally stops tapping. I guess I'm the one who has shocked and awed.

"So that's it then, isn't it? All this time with me and the reason you won't talk about your father is that you're afraid you'll end up like him," he says.

More silence passes between us, him waiting, me having

nothing else to say. It's the first and only time I've ever felt uncomfortable in his presence. But maybe that's a good thing.

"Hey, doc?" I ask.

"Yes?" he says.

"I think next session I'd like to tell you about my father," I say.

Dr. Russell lets the smallest smile find its way to the surface. He's been waiting to hear those words for a long time. But I have a feeling I need to tell someone else first.

"I think that'd be great," he says. "I look forward to it."

"I'm going to go now," I say. "I have to go buy a new suit."

"For what?" he asks.

"I have a dance to attend." *And a heart to win back.*

## OH NO

### THEA

Ethan straightens his bowtie in the car for the fourth time, but I don't say anything. I know if I did, it would make him even more nervous than he already is. But from a mother's perspective, he looks so much older than he is right now.

Today was all about getting ready for the school dance. He asked for a new haircut and putty to put in his hair. Of course, he insisted on trying to apply it by himself, and let's just say that ended with him having to wash his hair a second time. After that, he agreed to let me help.

We also got him new dress shoes, black slacks, and a button-up white shirt. I rolled up the sleeves for a more casual and cool look. Coupled with the suspenders and black bowtie, I'd say our teamwork has him looking quite dapper.

As his mom, I'm both incredibly proud and also trying not to cry my eyes out. He's growing up so fast, I feel like if I blink I'll miss something.

"Did you get the flowers?" he asks me, his voice suddenly panicked.

"Yes, buddy, they're in the back," I say. "Don't worry, we have everything."

We pull up to the school a couple of minutes later and my stomach flops. I don't think it's excitement. It doesn't feel that hopeful. If I had to put words to it, I'd say it's a nagging reminder that I wasn't supposed to be here alone tonight.

It's been over a week and I still haven't heard from him. Did I think for a split second that he'd show up at my door earlier and apologize and accompany me to this dance? Yes. Yes, I did. Did I also think about asking him if maybe we could be sex buddies? Yes. Yes, I also did think about that. I'm not ashamed to admit it's the greatest sex of my existence.

Ultimately, he told me the deal and I have to move on from it. I can't tangle myself up all over again. Especially not tonight.

Ethan grabs the flowers he picked for Ava from the back seat and the two of us walk toward the entrance.

"There's Ava," he says, breaking from my pace and running ahead.

In the distance, I search for a moment as my heart skips a beat. But Hanson isn't with her. I do see the familiar faces of Hawk and Drew, though.

"Hi," I say, holding my hand out to Drew. "I'm so glad you guys could make it." And I am. Sort of. Would it have been nice to look ahead and see Hanson standing here with Ava? Yes. Or no. Maybe. I don't know. But I know my heart did a sinking thing when it wasn't him, so there's that.

"Ava has been very excited today," Drew says. "She had Will do her hair and apply a little makeup and we took her out to find a new dress."

"Mom, don't say that," Ava says, looking over in embarrassment.

Leaning in toward Drew, I confess to her about Ethan's routine today. We all share a quiet giggle as Ethan gives Ava her flowers.

"I'll put those in the car," Hawk says. "Meet you all inside."

"Let's go, guys," Drew says, ushering us all inside. "And by the way, I love that dress."

Drew looks at me as she says this, causing me to look down at the light blue dress I pulled from further back in my closet. Keeping in mind I needed something appropriate for school, this seemed like a good choice. The straps are thicker, and the front isn't plunging at all. It still hugs my frame down to my waist. Then layers of tulle flow down to just below my knee. I paired it with clear heels and a black necklace.

Honestly, the whole ensemble makes me feel like a modern-day Cinderella. All I'm missing are those ball gown gloves and a pumpkin. Just because I'm here alone doesn't mean I can't look pretty for myself.

The kids ditch us once we make it into the gym, which has been transformed into a spectacular dance floor if I'm being honest. The decorating committee went above and beyond, draping all the walls in silky fabric and stringing hundreds of lights overhead. There are so many that you can't even see the rafters above.

Drew and I make our way to the concessions, grabbing a cup of punch from the bowl. We're joined a few minutes later by Hawk, who immediately cradles his wife's back and gives her a quick kiss. If I had to describe them to someone who's never met them, the only words that come to mind are "Alternative Tattooed Ken and Barbie". Or maybe "Badass Ken and Barbie". Either way, the point is, they're perfection mixed with a certain coolness that draws people in.

"I want to thank you guys for being able to come and chaperone," I say. "I know you've had a lot going on lately, so I appreciate it."

"Oh, it's no problem at all," Drew says. "We were itching to get just a few moments away from all of it. And honestly, his mom's recovery is going well so we're hiring a nurse to take evening shifts so we can get back to normal."

"Yeah, my mother is making us," Hawk says. "She says we're hovering."

"That sounds about right," I say, laughing.

"Now, if you'll excuse us, I promised this woman a dance," Hawk says, taking Drew by the hand to lead her onto the dance floor.

Oh to be that in love. I watch as they find an opening right in the middle of the action and a slow song begins to play as if on cue. Like I said. Perfection.

I scan the room, simultaneously checking on everything and looking for my son. He's not much for dancing, so when my eyes find him swaying to the song with his hands on Ava's waist like the little gentleman I raised him to be, my heart all but bursts from my chest. They're both smiling at each other and exchanging words I can't hear. But I like to think they're filled with kindness and affection. Well, age-appropriate affection.

From the corner of my eye, there's movement at the gym door and as I turn to check it out, I stop breathing. In the doorway, Hanson stands, his hands tucked into the pockets of a dark suit. He's staring at me and now I'm staring back and I don't know if I should just stay on this side of the punch bowl where it feels safe or if I need to move.

"Go on," Drew says, suddenly by my side. "The punch isn't going anywhere. Go on, girl."

She all but shoves me in Hanson's direction. My feet feel like they're moving much slower than I want them to. Slowly and all at once, I'm standing in front of him.

"What are you doing here?" I hold my breath. This is just the sort of earth-shattering moment I didn't prepare for tonight.

## FIND MY OWN WAY
### HANSON

I know I should say something. She's waiting for me to answer her and all I can think about is how lovely she looks in the multi-colored lights filtering into the hallway from the gym. But I can't tell her that. It's not the right thing to say at this moment, even if it seems like it might be.

"I have to tell you something," I finally say.

"Okay," she says, crossing her arms in front of her.

The singular act nearly breaks me. Thea's not doing it in anger. Her body language is full of hesitation. She's protecting herself. From me. Not physically of course, but from the words I might say. Here goes nothing.

"The first memory I can recall from my childhood is walking in on my father as he choked my mother. When he saw me, he stopped. My mother caught her breath and walked me to my room, assuring me she was fine and it was nothing," I say.

Thea's arms drop ever so slightly as her face contorts.

"My mother wore turtlenecks nearly all the time. My father was the type of man who only hit her in places she could cover up. Never the face," I say.

Shock rolls across Thea's face but I press on.

"Everyone thinks my mother died of a drug overdose. And drugs indeed killed her. But it was my father that took her life. Day by day, a little at a time. He chipped away at her soul until she was hollow. I know she thought about trying to run away, to take me with her. I know she daydreamed about the two of us disappearing somewhere he couldn't find us. But one time I heard him tell her that if she ever left, he'd cut both our throats," I say, my voice cracking.

Thea's hand finds my forearm, squeezing it. Her eyes are wide and glossy as she continues to stare up at me.

"He wanted me to be like him, to take over the family business. He's powerful and has a lot of people in his pocket. Let's just say his business dealings are more like criminal masterminding. There wasn't anything criminal going on in Rio that he didn't know about," I say, catching my breath. "My mother died so she could be free and there isn't a part of me that is angry at her for it. He never laid a hand on me and she knew that. She knew at the very least I would be physically okay after she was gone."

"Why are you telling me all of this?" Thea asks.

"Because," I say, my voice louder than I mean. "Because you need to understand who I am and what I'm made of before you decide."

"But-"

I cut her off. "Because I love you."

Thea's face twists with surprise and shock. She doesn't say anything in return, as I continue.

"Because I've never wanted to tell anyone any of this. But the truth is, I waited patiently until I was a little older. I plotted and collected evidence. All kinds. I snuck out and took the bus to the police station and I reported all of it. They called federal agents in, and that was the end of it. I was put into protective custody and eventually sent to live here with my aunt. I never saw him again," I say.

"Have you talked to him since?" she asks.

"Sometimes he writes me letters," I say. "I opened the first few but then I stopped. He's not serving a life sentence. He will get out one day. And sometimes I'm terrified of what that means for me or anyone close to me."

Thea swallows hard, feeling the full weight of everything I've said and what it all means. The last part is particularly alarming, I imagine. Not that I blame her.

"I look exactly like him, you know," I say. "I grew out my hair and started getting tattoos in an effort to not see him when I look in the mirror."

She leans in toward me, her hand cupping my jawline.

"And I'm frightened. His blood is my blood. He lives inside me. What if I'm like him? What if my hands could do what his have?" I ask.

At this moment, I begin to break. I can feel the tears beginning to erupt as I tuck my head into the crook of her neck, inhaling her scent after too long without it.

"It's okay," she whispers. "I've got you, it's okay."

My arms wrap around her as we stand there for several minutes, holding each other under the darkness I've unleashed.

"I'm sorry," I say.

"Don't be sorry," she says. "I asked for this. I wanted you to let me in. Never be sorry for that."

"It's a lot, I know," I say. "And given what I'd told you, I understand if it makes it impossible for you to trust me."

"Listen," she says. "You're right, that's a lot of shit. I can't believe you've been carrying that around by yourself all this time. It must be so heavy on you. And given what you've said, I understand why you don't want to share this with people. But..." Her voice trails off.

Her face is a wave of emotion I can't place. She bites her bottom lip as her eyes meet mine.

"But I love you too," she says. "And I know that's crazy because it hasn't even been that long but I don't care."

"Are you serious?" I ask in disbelief.

"What can I say? You're my penguin. Or my honeybee. Or my turkey. My lion. I just want you. And I don't think you'll ever be capable of what your father did because you don't want to be like him," she says. "That's not who you are. It never will be."

Thea takes my hand, placing it over her heart. Then, she places her hand over mine.

"Do you feel that?" she asks.

I nod. "Yes."

"When you spoon me, I can feel your heart beating against my back. And I can feel the exact moment my heart slows to match yours. For a few minutes, it feels like we exist as one. Our breathing matches up, along with our hearts. We sound like a single person. And there's no way the person who makes me feel that way could ever be a monster. Not now, not ever," she says.

"I love you," I whisper.

"I love you too," she says.

I close my eyes, pressing my forehead against hers as we begin to gently sway, our hands still on each other's chests. We're dancing. Despite the moment, I can't help but think of the Albatross. These birds come back year after year and dance with several partners until they trim their list down to just one. One partner. Once they find her, that's it. Albatross spend a great deal of time looking for the perfect mate. And their dance—the one performed between them during these sessions—is specific to that couple.

I found her. The woman whose heart beats in time with mine. My dancing partner. My lioness. My *deusa*. She freed me.

For as long as she'll have me, I belong to her.

# EPILOGUE
## BRIGHTSIDE

THEA

Aside from what's about to take place in approximately five minutes or so, nothing else matters. I'm about to witness one of the purest acts of love in existence and I can hardly contain myself.

Even Ethan is staring forward with excitement written all over his face. He and Ava have been a "couple" ever since the dance. According to reliable sources, he kissed her on the cheek and they held hands. So, for him, today is extra exciting.

"All rise for the honorable Judge Mackie," an officer in the corner calls out.

Hanson squeezes my hand as everyone in the wooden pews of the courtroom stands at attention. His smile is bright as he looks from me to his friend.

Hawk, Drew, Ava, and Knox are all positioned at the front

of the courtroom. Behind them, we stand along with Derek and Will to our right. To our left, Avery and Helena hold hands. Behind us, Jericho and Kate stand next to Hawk and Derek's mother. We're all here for this momentous occasion. The excitement is palpable, thick in the air but so sweet.

No one cares that the air conditioning in this room is barely working. No one cares about the noise of people waiting for their case numbers to be called. No one cares because what's about to happen is so much more important than anything else.

Judge Mackie calls for the matter of Ava Ashby, verifying various details, including Hawk's full name, and confirms that he does want to adopt Ava as his own. Hawk replies to each question exactly as he's supposed to. Then the judge turns to Ava.

"Do you want this man to be your dad?" he asks her.

Ava tells him that's what she wants, and then he confirms her name is now Ava Tanner. A few moments later, the gavel comes down and there's an eruption of clapping from the crowd.

"I can't believe it," I say. "I'm so happy."

"Can I ask you a question?" Hanson says.

"Of course," I say.

"How do you feel about having more kids?" he asks.

At first, the question throws me off guard, although I guess these types of thoughts do present themselves when you've just witnessed what we did. I think what's most surprising is my answer.

"For a long time, I didn't think I wanted more," I say, pausing. "But yes, I want more now."

"Good," he says. "Because I'd like to put a baby in you."

I choke. "Excuse me? Like right now?"

"No, my love. Not right now. This room is pretty crowded, I think someone would notice," he says.

I laugh. "You know what I mean."

"Of course, *deusa*," he says. "You can pick a time if you like."

"Well, you're going to have to marry me first," I say.

"Is that a proposal?" he asks.

My mouth hangs open. "Absolutely not. I want the real deal."

"How did Shane propose? Because I would like to do the exact opposite," he says, laughing.

"He didn't," I say. "I was already very pregnant, and one day he just walks in and tells me we're getting married before the baby comes."

"Which is why you want the real deal proposal, I'm guessing," he says.

"I've just never gotten one," I say. "It's something I'd like to experience."

"And so you shall, *deusa*," he says, leaning in to kiss me before we turn to exit the courtroom.

"Wait, you're serious? This isn't one of those times we're just casually talking about what could be in the future?" I ask.

Hanson's lips curl into that devilish grin he preserves only for very special occasions. Every time he does it, delicious knots form low in my belly. Though, I'm not sure what that smile is doing in this conversation. It seems a little out of context.

Once we've walked through the crowd and found our way to the sidewalk outside, he turns to me.

"I'm very serious, Thea," he says. "I love you. And I know we still haven't been together that long, but I want you to know I'm thinking about the future. Our future together."

"I love you," I say, pressing my lips to his.

"I love you too," he says as he pulls away from the kiss. "And maybe we're not ready for marriage or a baby, but that doesn't mean there isn't something we could do."

Tilting my head toward him, I squint my eyes as I try to read his facial expression. "What do you mean?"

Hanson reaches into his pocket for something, shielding it from my view.

"Hold out your hand," he says. "And close your eyes."

Though I'm still unsure what all this is about, I do as instructed.

"Thea James, you make me happier than I ever thought I could be. Moments spent not in your presence wound me. And while this isn't a proposal of marriage, it is one that would bring us much closer together," he says.

Hanson drops something into my hand, but I can't detect what it is.

"Open your eyes," he says.

When I look down at my palm, a single silver-colored key rests at its center.

"Will you move in with me?" he asks. "Both of you."

My mouth drops open as I look from the key to his face to the key again. Then, I look toward Ethan, who's smiling back at me.

"He's the man of your house, I asked him first," Hanson says.

My head spins back. "You did?" Tears brim my eyes as he nods again.

"Yes," I say. "Of course, yes."

Hanson envelops me in a hug, reaching for Ethan as well. All three of us stand on the sidewalk hugging as Ethan cheers and I sob and Hanson laughs. Honestly, I don't know whose reaction is more appropriate.

"We're going to be a family," Ethan says.

The moment the words leave his mouth, I'm a goner. All I've ever wanted is for Ethan to feel like he has a family. A whole family. These days, his father sees less and less of him and it kills my soul a little.

Hanson is a good man. He's kind, intelligent, and funny. I know he's afraid of failing in this role, but I'm not. I have enough faith in him for the both of us. It's a big step and I'm relieved to know he already spoke to Ethan about it himself. The pair have become very close. Each time Shane bails, Hanson swoops in with a fun activity or movie night or something to distract him from the disappointment.

Watching them do simple things like play a video game or make food together warms my heart in a way I can't explain. It's become a favorite pastime of mine.

The point is, I know we're going to be okay. The past be damned. The present is being thoroughly enjoyed. And the future is wholly unknown. But I know no matter what, there's someone in my corner. Finally.

And wouldn't you know it? He's everything I never knew I wanted.

## EPILOGUE

### MINE WOULD BE YOU

**HANSON**

This morning, I left the house with Ethan and told Thea we were going to get donuts but that's a lie. He and I have been planning today for months and we're finally ready.

We do pick up a donut box, though. That's part of the plan. You wouldn't think walking into a donut shop and asking to pay for an empty box would be a big deal, but they were very confused. I even offered to pay for a dozen but just take the box. In the end, though, they helped a guy out and just gave it to me.

Next, we make a stop at the jeweler to pick up the ring. That's right. It's time. Did I ever think I would be here in my life? No way. But that hasn't stopped me from fully embracing my role and that includes giving Thea a real proposal like she wants.

Upon further investigation, she doesn't want it like Will and Derek. No big party full of friends and family. It's not that she doesn't love them, but according to her, she wants something more intimate. And how did I do this investigative work, you ask? By making her go out and drink with Will and Drew, who reported back about their "girl talk". Maybe I should feel bad about that, but I'm actually pretty proud of my stealthiness.

Ethan carefully opens the donut box and uses double-sided tape to adhere the ring box to the center. It's then that I wonder if maybe we should have left some donuts surrounding it, but it's too late to make adjustments.

When we arrive back home, it's go time. Ethan carries the donut box in as I trail behind him. He makes a beeline for the kitchen and places it on the counter exactly where he's supposed to.

"Thea, you want a donut?" I call out.

From somewhere upstairs, I hear her yell down that she's coming. This is it. Am I nervous? Fuck yes. Do I feel like I want to puke? Also yes. But at this point, I'll just have to choke it back down.

Her footsteps fall on the stairs and it feels like it's taking her forever to get down here. Ethan is patiently sitting at the kitchen table but upon further inspection, his leg is bouncing at a record high speed beneath the table.

"What kind did y'all get?" she asks, finally entering the kitchen.

"An assortment," Ethan says quickly.

As she steps toward the box, I quietly walk up behind her and kneel.

Thea opens the lid, a loud gasp escaping her before her hands cover her mouth.

"Oh my god," she says, turning toward me. "What's happening right now?"

"Thea James," I say. "It's been a wild ride so far, full of a fair amount of obstacles. But also more love and partnership than I deserve. I can't imagine meeting another human being who makes me as happy as you make every single day. And if you'll have me, I'm yours. Forever. Will you marry me?"

Her glossy eyes spill tears down her cheeks as she collapses onto me, hugging my neck and kissing me.

"Yes," she says. "Yes, times infinity."

"Did you just say times infinity?" I ask, laughing.

"I teach sixth graders, what do you expect?" she asks.

Ethan begins clapping in the background, his excitement barely contained.

"Finally," he says.

"Here, give me your finger," I say, holding my hand out.

I slide the diamond ring onto her finger as she stares down in awe. I like to think I did a pretty good job choosing a ring she'd like. Honestly, it's not as easy as you'd think. There are a lot of options out there.

For a single moment in all this happiness, I think of my mother. There have been so many times I've wished she was here to see who I've become. Her name was Camila. And I know in my heart she would have loved Thea and Ethan too. It's in knowing this that I find peace.

Thea's face is lit up with the force of all the stars in the sky. My lioness. If ever a creature walked this earth that could be called divine, it's her.

I exist to worship her. It's my purpose in life. And I can think of nothing else that would satisfy my soul the way she does.

# ACKNOWLEDGMENTS

I'd like to thank the academy—wait. That's the wrong speech. Let me find my notes right quick. Ah yes.

I'm not going to lie. This was a rough one. During this release, I faced many personal obstacles that made this book nearly impossible to write. As I type this, it's after midnight and I lost my voice. I've pretty much been living on cough drops for two weeks. So special thanks to Cynthia, Trish, and Cary who all sent me wellness packages. You guys are lifesavers.

So firstly, I want to acknowledge myself. I don't think I've ever done that. Through blood, sweat, tears, and congestion, I did it. And I'm proud of myself. I'm proud of this entire series. It's truly changed my life.

To be writing the final acknowledgements in the final book of this series is bittersweet.

Thank you to Jen Rogue for always being by my side. To Cynthia, Kayleigh, and Shannon for being in my corner. And an extra shoutout to Shannon for being the best damn PA I could have ever imagined. She literally keeps this thing running, y'all.

Thank you to my beta readers, Ashleigh, Al, Daniele, and

Leah. Your notes were super helpful and I couldn't have done it without you.

Thank you to my agent, Savannah, at Two Daisy, who works so hard to get my books everywhere. The day I signed on with you changed my life.

Thank you to Shauna at Wildfire Marketing. We've been working together on releases for nearly two years now and she's nothing short of amazing.

I guess this is where I add a thanks to my kids, even though they still don't do anything. Yesterday, my daughter came in just to ask me if I could smell something. She didn't even bring me snacks either. It's like what the hell, get out, I don't want to smell random things for you.

Thank you to my partner, Chris. He's been wonderful for the past several months. Very helpful and supportive. I couldn't ask for a better person to conquer the world with. He loves three kids who aren't his own and I don't think there's anything else to say about that. P. S. I love you.

Is that it? Oh shit. No. Lastly, thank you to every single person who has picked up Hawk and been sucked into this series. I truly wouldn't be where I am right now without you. I hope you have enjoyed every moment of this series. Thank you a million times for falling in love with the Men of Bird's Eye.

## ALSO BY KAT SAVAGE

### *POETRY*

*Mad Woman*

*Anchors & Vacancies*

*Let Me Count The Ways*

*All The Things I Said*

*Counting Backwards From Gone*

*I Hope This Makes You Uncomfortable*

*Letters From A Dead Girl*

### *NOVELS*

*Standalone Novels*

*For Now*

*With This Lie*

*A Chance at Love Series*

*A Fighting Chance*

*One More Chance*

*Taking A Chance*

*Men Of Bird's Eye Series*

*Hawk*

*Will*

*Avery*

## ABOUT THE AUTHOR

Kat Savage resides in Louisville, Kentucky with her three beautiful children, her hunky spouse, and three spoiled ass dogs. She secretly has hopes of getting chickens one day.

She was driven to write out of a need for distraction and self-preservation after the death of her sister in 2013. Since then, it's snowballed into a full blown passion she can't escape. Even on the toughest days, she wouldn't want to. Her unique brand of storytelling ranges from tragic poetry to swoony rom coms and even a little darkness. She uses her real life experiences to fuel every word she puts on paper. She's published several collections of poetry and multiple novels.

Savage is a natural storyteller, getting better with each book. She tries to give the characters in her novels depth, whether they're serious or comical. Savage builds them in layers with the hope that you see a little of yourself in some of them.

www.thekatsavage.com
Newsletter